Ransom's Mark

DAUGHTERS OF THE FAITH SERIES

Ransom's Mark

A STORY BASED ON THE LIFE OF THE YOUNG PIONEER OLIVE OATMAN

Wendy Lawton

MOODY PUBLISHERS

CHICAGO

All Scripture quotations are taken from the King James Version.

Published in association with Books & Such Literary Management.

Edited by Cessandra Dillon
Interior design: Erik M. Peterson
Cover design: Jeff Miller, Faceout Studio
Cover illustration and portrait: Kelsey Fehlberg
Cover watercolor wash 1 copyright © 2021 by 8H/Shutterstock (1720194910).
Cover watercolor wash 2 copyright © 2021 by TairA/Shutterstock (274620503).
Cover texture copyright © 2021 by titoOnz/Shutterstock (713253826).
All rights reserved for all of the above backgrounds/textures.

ISBN: 978-0-8024-3638-2

Printed by Bethany Press in Bloomington, MN—11/21

Originally delivered by fleets of horse-drawn wagons, the affordable paperbacks from D. L. Moody's publishing house resourced the church and served everyday people. Now, after more than 125 years of publishing and ministry, Moody Publishers' mission remains the same—even if our delivery systems have changed a bit. For more information on other books (and resources) created from a biblical perspective, go to www.moodypublishers.com or write to:

Moody Publishers
820 N. LaSalle Boulevard
Chicago, IL 60610

11 13 15 17 19 20 18 16 14 12

Printed in the United States of America

For Patrick

Contents

1

Seeing the Elephant

O live!"
The sun was barely up. Why was Lucy shaking her? And what was the commotion outdoors? Olive remembered waking to barking dogs during the night, but before she could work out what was happening, it was morning and her sister Lucy was dragging off the coverlet.

"Get up. Get dressed. Help Mary Ann get ready. And then get Charity Ann dressed. We have company."

"Company?" Olive stretched, reaching her arms way above her head and extending her toes as far as they'd point. How could they have company this early? Their cabin stood on an isolated Illinois homestead a full five miles outside Fulton. It wasn't on the way to anything.

"Yes, you lay-abed, we have company," Lucy said, excitement tingeing her words. "The Wheelers and the Pounds stopped late last night on their way from New York to the

West." Lucy gave Olive one final shake before leaving. "You must get up. I need to help Ma and the ladies prepare breakfast. Lorenzo is chopping wood, and Royce is helping him."

Olive threw off the coverlet and sat on the side of her bed, lifting the edge of the curtain and peeking out the window. The yard teemed with activity. Two canvas-covered wagons had pulled in the yard during the night. It looked like a regular frolic with children running, dogs barking, and Pa standing by the wagons talking with two men.

Had they brought those wagons all the way from East Bloomfield? New York seemed so far away, almost like another country. Olive remembered that her mother and father had been married in East Bloomfield.

Once, when Pa and Lorenzo were away, Ma told the girls all about her wedding in the old East Bloomfield Congregational Church. She had carefully lifted her watered silk wedding dress out of the chest. As Ma told them all about the day, she let Lucy, Olive, and Mary Ann unfold the gown, showing them the puffy gigot sleeves and the heavily weighted skirt. She unrolled her Mary Stuart cap and the delicate lace ruff from the linen in which they were lightly rolled. The lace was so fine it looked like cobwebs. Ma confided that she had waited to marry until the very end of April in the hope that the lilacs would force a bloom. The wedding supper had been at the home of the Wheelers.

Why, it must be the same Wheelers who were whooping it up in their yard!

Olive woke her little sister, Mary Ann. Putting a finger over her lips, Olive pointed Mary Ann toward the outhouse. Normally the girls would have taken care of their entire toilette in their room, but Olive didn't relish having to clean the slops bucket while company visited. The girls managed to slip back inside before anyone saw them.

Olive poured water from the pitcher into the basin. She washed, wrung the cloth out, and repeated the procedure, helping Mary Ann wash up.

"Do we wear our Sunday dresses, Olive?" Mary Ann loved her new Sunday dress.

"No. I think we have work to do. Let's wear our next-to-best dresses." She put a pinafore over Mary Ann's and an apron over her own. "Can you tidy up the room while I take care of Charity Ann?"

"Oh dear, I can't empty the basin." Of late, the words "oh dear" had peppered much of Mary Ann's conversation. She overheard a neighbor use the phrase and had enthusiastically adopted it.

"We'll leave it for now." In a large family, they'd long ago learned to pitch in and help each other out. They'd also learned that taking care of people came first and chores must sometimes go by the wayside.

Olive readied three-year-old Charity Ann for the day. She would follow Olive the rest of the day.

"Olive Ann." Ma followed her out onto the doorstep, setting the white glazed stoneware crock on the step along with her pair of pruning shears. "Fill this crock with lilacs, will you? When you are finished, put it on the table that Lucy and Lorenzo are setting up under the oak."

Lucy and Lorenzo had laid a pair of wide boards across two sawhorses, and Lucy was smoothing one of Ma's best Belgian linen tablecloths over the makeshift table. Some of the other young people carried dishes and utensils to the table.

Olive hurried to cut an armful of lilacs. Ma's lilac bush scented the entire yard, and, despite the early hour, Olive had to gently brush bees away as she cut. They started work early when lilac nectar scented the air. She remembered to scrape the blade along the woody stems before putting them into the crock so the lilacs could soak water deep into the marrow of their flesh. When she couldn't squeeze another stem into the crock, she carried the lilacs to the center of the table and went to fetch water to fill the crock.

"Why, Mary Ann Sperry!" One of the women carrying out a platter of flapjacks stopped short of the table. "I mean . . . Mrs. Oatman." The woman blushed to have resorted to Ma's maiden name.

"Whatever is wrong, Mrs. Wheeler?" Ma looked concerned.

"Nothing is wrong, but, I declare, if that doesn't look like the exact same crock of lilacs you used to set on your table in New York."

"It's most nearly the same," Ma said with a laugh, putting small pitchers of syrup on the table. "The crock is the salt-glazed one your folks gave me as a wedding gift, and that lilac bush was started from a slip off a slip off a slip of my grand-mother's bush from the Berkshires."

"Well, I'll be . . ." Mrs. Wheeler said. "How did you manage that?"

"My mother started one off grandmother's bush. When Mr. Oatman and I set out to move west, Mother gave me a slip off hers. It was wrapped in moss and tied with linen. I kept it moistened during the whole journey. By the time we reached LaHarpe, it was already well rooted. I left the moss and the linen around the root ball and set it into the ground."

Olive couldn't help seeing the sadness around Ma's eyes when she spoke of LaHarpe. Many a dream had died there.

"How did you move the bush from LaHarpe way out here to the country?"

"We didn't move the bush. In fact, we've left a lilac bush at every place we've alighted on this journey."

Ma motioned for the men to come sit down with the la-dies. Lucy and Olive shooed all the children into the house to eat around the big kitchen table. After they got plates filled and little ones settled, they took food out to the big boys, sitting near the back door. Between mouthfuls, they replen-ished the platter of flapjacks on the adult table.

Ma flashed them a grateful look. They could see weariness in the set of her shoulders. Any day now she was expecting the seventh Oatman child.

"So, when you left LaHarpe, where did you go?" Mrs.

Wheeler was intent on catching up with all the years she'd missed.

"You do know we lost our mercantile in the depression of 1842, don't you?" Pa spoke quietly but seemed relieved to get the words out.

"Why, no, Royce, we did not know." Mr. Wheeler seemed uncomfortable and gave a look to his wife that seemed to fault her for prying.

"Too many folk lost everything," Mr. Pound said. He quietly folded his napkin. "You must be right proud to have built up another farm and taken such good care of your family."

Pa seemed to relax. "Thank you for that. It hasn't been easy. When we lost the store, we first went back to Pennsylvania to be near relations. The only things we took with us were our household belongings."

"And a slip off my lilac bush," Ma said smiling. "Does anyone care for more coffee?" She looked toward Lucy who carried the big graniteware pot steaming with freshly brewed coffee.

Olive began clearing plates as Lucy poured and the adults visited.

"We didn't stay long in Pennsylvania," Pa said. "The wide open spaces of the West had already settled in our blood, and it was too late to be satisfied back in the East."

"And you two coming from such established Yankee stock?" Mrs. Pound pretended to be shocked. "Mrs. Oatman, don't I recall that your Sperry kin settled in Connecticut just a few years after the Mayflower landed?"

Ma laughed. "You don't think those fine Yankees ventured all the way from England to land on these shores because they were content to stay at home, do you?"

Olive could see Pa squeeze Ma's hand under the table.

"Mrs. Oatman is right," Pa said. "We both have a touch of wanderlust in us. We left Pennsylvania and made the trip out West again. I had to teach school in Chicago for a time to save enough to homestead a piece of land and start all over. We finally ended up here in Fulton."

Ma touched the lilacs on the table. "I went over to our old place in LaHarpe and snipped a piece of the Sperry lilac. When it sprouted, I knew we were home again."

"We met your children last night," Pa said. "Let us introduce you to our family." He signaled to the children to come. Charity Ann was already following Olive again. "This is our eldest daughter, Lucy. She is 16 now and a great help to her mother."

Lucy gave a proper curtsy.

"This is Lorenzo, he's 14; Olive Ann is 12; Royce here is 9; Mary Ann is 6; and Charity Ann is 3."

No one mentioned the soon-to-be-expected baby since a person never mentioned such things in polite society. It was one of those things one pretended not to notice.

The younger children ran off to play.

Olive hovered nearby to offer coffee or to clear things off the table. Charity Ann dogged her every step.

As Olive poured coffee into Mrs. Wheeler's cup, the woman turned to Ma and said, "I declare, Mrs. Oatman, if I didn't know Olive was your daughter, I'd say I was looking at you twenty years ago."

"Yes," agreed Mrs. Pound. She turned to Olive. "Did you know your mama was reckoned to be the beauty of Ontario County?"

The comment made both Ma and Olive blush.

"Olive has her father's shiny dark hair, but those intense eyes and fine features are pure Sperry." Mrs. Wheeler seemed not to notice Olive's discomfort at being singled out. "And how ever does she keep that lovely fair skin living out here on the prairie?"

Lucy was the one most people accounted a beauty because she had Pa's round face and Ma's light-colored hair. Mary Ann favored the Oatman side as well, though she was of a frailer build. Little C. A. was simply a cherub of a girl, as Olive always liked to say. And the boys? Well . . . they were boys. Olive thought Lorenzo a taller version of their father, serious-looking and solid. He was the one who always looked out for his sisters. You could always count on Lorenzo. Royce was a round, playful, rosy-cheeked version of his mother.

"So tell us about your journey," Pa prompted the men, anxious to change the subject.

"All we hear about in the East is the opportunity in the West," Mr. Pound said.

"Mr. Horace Greeley, the editor of the *New York Tribune,* has been hammering us with editorial after editorial. Surely you've heard his famous words, even out here on the prairie . . ." Mr. Wheeler put a serious look on his face, puffed out his chest and said, "Go west, young man. Go west."

"Yes, and we've not only read his words, we've seen wagon load after wagon load heeding the call." Pa stood up to stretch his legs. "Where will you go?"

"We are going to take the Oregon Trail," Mr. Pound said. "At least that's the plan. We will head for Council Bluffs. That's where we'll rendezvous, purchase all our supplies, and join up with a wagon train."

Ma and the ladies stood up and shook out their skirts. They picked up the last of the dishes and went into the house to begin planning dinner. Since there were no children her age, Olive stayed close to the table so she could hear the talk of the West. The men talked about word of a gold rush in California and land to be had for the taking. They discussed the different routes and the best time of the year to start.

Olive watched her father as he listened to his friends. They pored over Mr. Wheeler's copy of *The Emigrant's Guide to California.* They walked over to the wagons, and she could see Pa running appreciative hands along the canvas stretched over the ribs and squatting down to look at the strength of the axles. By the time the women had dinner prepared in the early afternoon, Olive saw a yearning in her father's face.

During dinner, the men continued to talk about the journey west. The children ate and cleared away the dishes, and still the adults talked.

"Do you fear going?" Ma asked later, as the women and the girls worked to bake enough loaves of bread to hold them until they reached Council Bluffs.

"Sometimes," admitted Mrs. Wheeler. "But look at them." She pointed to the men. "Once they make up their minds to see the elephant, there is no stopping them."

"See the elephant?" Ma asked.

"It's a figure of speech. Remember when we were children and the circus came to town? We couldn't think about anything else until we had been able to see the elephant." Mrs. Wheeler sighed as she looked out the door at the three men earnestly examining the wagon wheels.

"You asked about fear, Mary Ann." Mrs. Pound lowered her voice and lapsed back into girlhood names. "The term 'to see the elephant' actually comes from a story of a farmer who came to town with his whole crop of vegetables in his wagon. He arrived just in time to see the circus parade being led by the elephant." She gave the bread dough a hearty thump on the floured board. "He was thrilled to see the parade, but his horses startled and bolted, overturning his wagon and spilling his entire load of vegetables into the ditch." She continued to knead as she talked. "When the townspeople expressed their regrets for his loss, he just slapped his thigh and said, 'I don't give a hang, for I have seen the elephant.'"

"Isn't that the truth," said Mrs. Wheeler. "Once a man's got a hankering to see the elephant, the cost doesn't seem to matter."

That night, they ate a supper of wild strawberries, crusty baked bread with newly churned butter, and glasses of cool milk. The grownups talked long into the night. The children continued to run and play in the dark, trying to trap fireflies and listening to the far-off sounds of wolves. Nobody stirred to put the children to bed—they sort of drifted off and fell asleep on one bed or another, hoping someone would eventually tuck them into the proper bed.

Early in the morning, before the sun had barely risen, the Pounds and the Wheelers packed the last of their things into the wagons and headed out of the Oatman yard. Children walked alongside the wagons, careful to stay to the side since the horses tied onto the back kicked up a lot of dust. The Oatmans walked alongside for a ways, calling out good-byes as they walked.

When Ma could no longer keep up, she called out, "God be with you, dear friends." When Ma said it, she meant it. She believed God walked with them every step of the way.

As the wagons pulled away, the Oatmans continued waving until all they could see was a cloud of dust on the horizon. Olive heard her mother sigh deeply and understood the reason —her father stood there staring after the wagons with a look of stark longing. At that moment, Olive knew the truth—Pa would not be satisfied until he saw the elephant for himself.

2

Wagons Ho

"Olive." Ma held out a piece of linen and a spongy clump of moss. "Cut about a six-inch stem off my lilac. Choose the healthiest branch near the tip. Soak the moss, and then use the linen to tie the damp moss around the cutting."

Ma went back inside to finish scrubbing every inch of their house. Olive couldn't understand what drove her mother to clean a house that would probably stay empty until dusty cobwebs festooned each rafter. When she asked, Ma simply looked at her in that way that said, "I don't wish to discuss this any further."

While Ma silently scrubbed, Pa hopped from one detail to the next—checking and oiling harnesses; running his hands over the legs of the horses; and checking his lists of provisions, farming implements, and bags of seeds.

Ever since the day spent with their Oregon-bound friends a year ago, Pa had seemed restless. At first Ma had been busy with the newest Oatman, an ever-hungry little boy, but, before long, Olive noticed that she became quiet and pensive when Pa complained about Illinois weather or the creep of civilization toward their homestead.

Four years ago, during their second year of farming at Fulton, Pa injured his back moving a boulder while helping a neighbor dig a well. The injury had bothered him ever since, especially in the extreme cold of winter. Sometimes when his back pained him it made his knee and the side of his foot tingle and become numb. Over the last four years, he'd worked around it, resting when the injury became inflamed and doubling up on the work when it subsided.

Last year, however, all Pa could talk about was how much the intense cold affected him.

"Mary Ann," Pa whispered. "Are you awake?"

Olive sometimes heard her parents talking long into the night.

"I fear that if I am to somehow live long enough to educate my family or even to enjoy tolerable health, we must make a move." When Ma didn't answer, he went on. "I need to seek a climate free from the extreme changes of weather."

Olive strained to hear Ma's answer.

After a long silence, Ma asked, "Does this have anything to do with all those strange pamphlets you've been discussing with Mr. Thompson and others about a colony—a promised land—near the Colorado River?"

"I don't know about 'strange.'" Father cleared his throat.

Olive recognized the gesture as the one her father always made before launching into a lecture or an argument. "I don't agree with all the beliefs of the man calling for this journey, but I do believe the destination to be a Promised Land—filled with tall grasses, abundant water, rich soil, and warm climate."

"I've never stood against you before, Royce, and I won't do so now. You've provided well for us over the years. The job God gave me is to follow your lead and care for this family." Ma laughed a quiet laugh. "Besides, for as long as I've known you, you seem to have an incurable tugging westward. I might as well be prepared to follow you to the edge of the Pacific Ocean and get it over with."

So that was that.

Pa began planning. Olive had never seen him so happy. When he finally sold everything, he announced that they had fifteen hundred dollars to outfit themselves for the journey and to make a new start near the Rio Colorado in California.

They purchased near home most of the things they needed for the journey. Pa knew that if he waited until they arrived in Independence, prices would triple. He bought a sturdy Studebaker wagon—the kind that pioneers called prairie schooners. A canvas bonnet covered the curved ribs of strong oak. The heavy bed of the wagon was tarred to make it water-tight so that it could float down a gentle stream if needed. The sideboards were beveled outward so that rainwater couldn't seep in between the bonnet and the bed.

A jockey box attached to the side of the wagon. Pa kept checking and rechecking to make sure he included every-thing they might need inside the box. It carried extra iron bolts, linch pins, skeins, nails, hoop iron, a variety of tools, and a jack. Also slung on the side of the wagon were two water barrels, a butter churn, a shovel and axe, a tar bucket, a feed trough for the livestock, and a chicken coop.

Ma packed the interior. She used every inch of space to bring as many of the family treasures as she could without weighing down the wagon. They needed clothing and yard-age goods to make more. She had to include all the cooking utensils needed to make meals along the trail, as well as the tools she'd need to set up housekeeping in California.

She tried to pack and discard without becoming sentimen-tal, but it was impossible. In the end, her family linens, the salt crock, her wedding dress, and all the family books were tucked into crevices in the wagon.

One of the last things to go into the wagon was the lilac cutting Olive had carefully prepared. Ma wanted it where she could keep it moist, so she placed the rooting end in a small oilcloth sack tied round with twine and set on the shelf near her Bible. She had also made an oilcloth sack for her Bible in case they took a drenching.

All the rest of the space held food supplies, farming im-plements, and bedding. Down the center of the wagon, Ma arranged a bed of sorts. She and the little ones would sleep in that nest, along with Lucy and Olive at times. It would be a tumble of bodies in a cramped space, but it provided safety and warmth.

Once they reached Independence, Pa hoped to buy a couple of small army surplus tents for extra sleeping. Until then, he, Lorenzo, and Royce planned to unroll their bedding under the box of the wagon.

They had a team of six oxen to pull the wagon and tied their two horses and a milk cow behind. As far as humanly possible, they were ready for the adventure ahead.

• • •

Pa took the Bible out of the oilcloth and opened it. "This passage comes from the thirty-third chapter of the book of Genesis." He looked down at the page and read, "And he said, Let us take our journey, and let us go, and I will go before thee." He closed the Bible and led them in prayer, asking God to walk alongside them on the journey.

The wagon rolled out of the Fulton homestead toward Davenport, Iowa, where they planned to meet up with their Illinois neighbors, the Thompsons, for the journey to Independence, Missouri—the jumping-off place to the West.

• • •

Independence teemed with activity. To Olive it seemed as if the whole country was headed west. It looked like the encampment of a vast army on wheels.

So many *emigrant* wagon train companies met up and pulled out of the town that the wagons either sank into dusty soil halfway to the axle in dry weather or got stuck in the thick clay mud they called "gumbo" after a rain.

The fields around the city had been stripped to bare dirt by hundreds of thousands of grazing cattle funneling through Independence. With thousands of campfires, not a twig of firewood survived in the entire region—every downed tree or broken branch became a treasure.

The Brewster Party—the one Pa had decided to join— agreed to meet four miles south of town. When all assembled, there were twenty wagons and fifty-two people in the party, most of them children. That suited Olive just fine. She hoped to find a girl her age, since Lucy's best friend, Susan Thompson from Fulton, traveled in the same party.

Olive met boys and babies, toddlers and little girls, but apparently she was the only 13-year-old girl. How she wished Pa could wait for a different wagon train, but she knew that the careful timing of their departure was critical. Had they planned to take the Oregon Trail, the Bozeman Trail, or the California Trail, they'd be obliged to wait until spring. The mountain passes would be closed by snow long before they could arrive. But, because they chose the southern route— the Santa Fe Trail to the Gila Trail—cold weather would not be as much a problem as heat and drought could be in the southern deserts.

"Want to walk over to that ridge with Susan and me?" Lucy asked.

Olive couldn't believe they would ask. She looked over toward Ma, nursing the baby. C. A. was taking a nap, and Royce and Mary Ann were playing with the other children. A moment before she had felt lonely—now she felt like skipping across the prairie.

"Yes. Let me get my bonnet." She ran to the wagon. Ma smiled with a quick wink of her eye. She understood the reason for Olive's sudden excitement.

Maybe this trip would be an adventure after all.

The girls walked to the ridge and found an outcropping of stone on which to sit.

"My pa says to enjoy these ridges and rock outcroppings while we have them," Susan said. "At times, the land will be so flat we'll not find a single spot offering privacy."

Olive knew what she meant by privacy. There would be no outhouses along wilderness trails. It was not just grooming privacy that they craved. Because of the time they'd already spent on the road from Davenport, Olive knew how important it could be to put a little space between you and a whole wagon train of people.

"Don't fret." Lucy laughed. "My mother already thought of that. She brought old blankets to tie between two trees to offer some little privacy on the plains."

Olive should have known Ma would think of a plan.

"And if there are no trees or scrub brushes tall enough,"

Lucy continued, "we'll tie our makeshift curtain between two wagons."

The girls giggled at the thought of some of the inconveniences they'd experience before they reached the Rio Colorado.

Susan changed the subject abruptly. "My cousin said that nothing makes hair softer and shinier than washing it in a cold running stream." Susan lowered her voice to a whisper. "And she said that if we find elderberries, we can crush them and stain our lips reddish."

Before Olive could say anything, both girls started laughing, and Olive realized Susan was teasing. Sort of. *Surely she wouldn't think of using face paint, would she?*

"Don't look so worried, sister," said Lucy. "Susan loves to talk nonsense."

The afternoon passed with light talk and laughter. They went back to the camp to spell their mothers with the little ones and to help prepare the meal. The first couple of nights they prepared a large communal meal for the whole *emigrant* party, but they soon settled into their trail routine of separating into family groups for meals.

That night, August 9, 1850, everyone gathered after supper to set regulations for the long trip west and to get acquainted with each other. Besides Mr. Brewster, who organized the party, the party consisted of Susan's family (the Thompsons), the Lane family, the Kelly family, the Wilders, the Metteers, the Brinshalls, the Oatmans, and others.

After the formalities concluded, Susan took out her violin to play. She started with "Money Musk" and "Zipp Coon." The dogs barked, the oxen stepped nervously, the children hopped, and some of the men grabbed their partners to dance. As the night wore on and the breeze picked up dust off the prairie and swirled around the revelers, Susan ended by playing "The Old Oaken Bucket." Every voice joined in singing the words:

> *How dear to my heart are the scenes of my childhood*
> *When fond recollection presents them to view,*
> *The orchard, the meadow, the deep tangled wildwood,*
> *And ev'ry loved spot which my infancy knew—*
> *The wide spreading pond, and the mill that stood by it,*
> *The bridge and the rock where the cataract fell;*
> *The cot of my father, the dairy house nigh it,*
> *And e'en the rude bucket that hung in the well.*
> *The old oaken bucket, the iron bound bucket,*
> *The moss covered bucket that hung in the well.*

Olive glanced at her mother to see the glisten of tears reflecting the moonlight. Ma pulled a handkerchief out of her apron pocket. Looking around the circle, it was apparent she was not alone.

> *The moss covered bucket I hailed as a treasure,*
> *For often at noon, when returned from the field,*

I found it the source of an exquisite pleasure,
The purest and sweetest that nature can yield.
How ardent I seized it, with hands that were glowing,
And quick to the white pebbled bottom it fell
Then soon, with the emblem of truth overflowing,
And dripping with coolness, it rose from the well.
The old oaken bucket, the iron bound bucket,
The moss covered bucket that hung in the well.

Susan put her violin away as someone led in prayer for a safe journey ahead. Families gathered sleepy children and headed off toward their wagons for the night.

Sleep was a long time in coming for Olive. She tried to be still, listening to the melody of the night—sounds of lowing cattle, soft nickers of horses, the far-off howl of the coyote, a chorus of sputters and snores, and the muffled weeping of a homesick pioneer. Eventually she must have fallen asleep, wedged tightly between Lucy and Mary Ann.

• • •

After morning prayers, Pa and Lorenzo hitched the oxen to the wagon as Ma and the girls finished cooking the food that must take them through the day. They wouldn't halt until suppertime. Olive hoped the tasks of getting underway would eventually become routine, but for now, they had to remember each step. Ma would handle the reins, if needed, and either Lucy or Olive would take turns inside the wagon caring for the baby and C. A. while the other walked. Mary Ann and Royce could walk alongside, play with their friends, or ride if they became tired.

When they first began to talk about the trip all those months ago, Olive figured the family would ride comfortably in the wagon from Fulton to California, just as they did in Illinois when they rode to church. She laughed now when she compared her expectation to reality.

The wagon weighed some 1,300 pounds empty. With all their belongings, supplies, and foodstuffs added, the prairie schooner lumbered along at a snail's pace. Most *emigrant* parties covered only about fifteen miles a day. Even when walking alongside, the pace seemed too slow. Children would spend the whole day running up ahead and running back to check on the wagon. The men of the party often rode on horseback, riding far ahead to scout the trail and coming back to check on the progress of the train. Olive guessed that much of the "scouting" took place because the men were vexed by the plodding pace.

Riding in the wagon bounced and jostled the passengers until they were bruised and sore. None of the axles on the Oatman covered wagon had springs—the only springs on the whole wagon were those under the driver's seat. The rutted dirt roads of the trail were regular washboards. Sometimes Olive thought her teeth would rattle out of her gums.

They hadn't been long on the road to Davenport when they found a purpose for the bumps and jumps. Ma discovered they could fill the butter churn with fresh milk in the morning, and, by night, they only had to pour off the buttermilk and they scraped out a lump of sweet yellow butter, ready for supper without any further churning.

And many a mother claimed that the jostling of the wagon cured a colicky baby. Olive knew it had the opposite effect on her—riding inside made her downright cranky.

But none of that mattered. It was August 10th and at long last, they were hitched, loaded, and ready. The children stood expectantly, as James Brewster raised his horn to his lips and let out a shrill note followed by the shout, "Wagons ho!"

One by one, the heavy wagons creaked, swayed, and rocked as they pulled out of the circle, straightening into a long line to stretch across the vast prairie.

Unexpectedly, Olive felt her scalp tighten and chills run across her shoulders. Just a moment before the trip had held promise of great adventure. What changed? What caused a jagged shard of fear to pierce the excitement? Olive tried to shake off the eerie feeling, but it persisted as the wagons moved farther away from the safety of home.

3

Storms Brewing

Despite Olive's momentary sense of dread, the first week passed in a cloud of dust and excitement. The wagon train rolled across the prairie as children played and families worked together. At night the wagons circled. Boys gathered wood or buffalo dung, which settlers called "prairie coal," to build the cooking fires. The men unhitched the teams and examined the oxen—running sensitive, probing hands over their sides to make sure the harnesses didn't rub sores on the animals. The women cooked, and the older girls cared for the children.

The second night, Olive, Lucy, and Susan took the little Oatmans and the little Thompsons down to the creek to wash off some of the dust before supper. Charity Ann seemed especially tired. She mostly wanted to suck her thumb, snuggle into Olive's lap, and stroke her braids.

"Ouch, I've got bug bites all over my legs," Susan said.

"Me too," Lucy said. "I figured out that if I walked farther away from the cattle, the biting flies weren't as bad."

"Nothing helps with these mosquitoes." Olive was swatting some of the biggest mosquitoes she'd ever seen. She could hear them humming near her ear. "They seem mighty hungry."

"Not as hungry as me," Royce said, putting out his arms and circling the girls in his imitation of a hungry mosquito. "Do you think Ma has supper ready?" Nothing ever seemed to fill that boy.

"Are you all washed up, Royce? We may be miles away from civilization, but Ma would see you starve before she'd let you come to the table with dirty hands."

Lucy helped Mary Ann wash off some of the trail dust. "Come here, Royce. Let me wipe your hands dry, and then you can take the towel to Olive."

Susan gathered the Thompson brood and herded them over to their wagon.

"Olive," said Lucy in a whisper. "Let's get the children back up to Mother and come back here after campfire tonight when the mosquitoes have gone to sleep."

"Please let me come, too," Mary Ann pleaded. "I'm big."

Olive almost said no until she remembered how she felt when Susan and Lucy included her. "If Ma says you can."

Lucy took Charity Ann from Olive's lap, and the Oatman children scrambled up the bank toward the smell of food. Olive could hear stomachs rumbling. Something about the trail made a body mighty hungry. They needed to be careful about rations on the trail, however. They could little afford the luxury of eating their fill as they had back in Illinois. Provisions needed to stretch until the end of the journey.

After supper, Ma bedded down the baby and Charity Ann while the rest of the family gathered around the campfire. At first, it was like the nights in Independence. Mr. Metteer brought out his harmonica, and everyone joined in on a rowdy singing of "Buffalo Gal."

"Enough frivolity," Mr. Brewster announced. "Let us begin a solemn discussion about theology and try to set a few things straight."

The-ol-uh-gee? Olive noticed several men exchange weary glances around the campfire, but no one argued with their leader. As Mr. Brewster began to drone on about "the literal meaning of the Promised Land," Susan, Lucy, Olive, and Mary Ann slipped off toward the creek.

"Oh, how I hope we don't have to listen to argumentation every night," Susan said as they followed the faint trail single file through the tall grass.

"After a long day traveling, it most likely will put everyone fast asleep." Lucy agreed, reaching out for Mary Ann's hand. The younger sister lagged behind Lucy, and Olive kept stepping on the back of Mary Ann's boots in the dark.

"Oh dear, it's dark here, isn't it?" Mary Ann said in a hushed voice, hurrying to add, "but I'm not scared."

The three older girls laughed, but Olive understood. She also felt the depth of the darkness. A deep stillness seemed to drown out the sound of the creek splashing over the rocks. The occasional plop of something falling into the water punctuated the rhythmic lapping of the water. Olive tried to convince herself it sounded like a bullfrog. Yes, it must be a bullfrog—a snake would soundlessly pierce the water with barely a ripple. Olive hated snakes.

"I wonder if animals come here to drink," Lucy said, squinting her eyes to try to peer into the darkness.

"What kinds of animals live out here on the prairie?" Susan asked. "I know buffalo do . . . and coyotes, foxes, and raccoons . . ."

"Do you think there are any panthers?" Olive looked hard into the darkness as they came to the creek bank. Tree branches stretched twiglike fingers over the creek. She could almost imagine the shape of a panther crouching on a sturdy limb near the trunk of the tree.

"You have such an imagination, Olive." Lucy tried for a light tone of voice as her eyes continued to scan the far bank.

Mary Ann scooted over next to Olive. "Oh dear, what about bears?"

"Do you see a forest around here, Mary Ann?" Lucy reached over and tweaked Mary Ann's nose. "If we keep this up, we'll end up scaring ourselves silly. Mostly there are hoot owls and trout and frogs and . . ."

A wild cry ripped through the quiet, and Mary Ann screamed and wrapped herself around Olive. Olive's imagination or not, it sounded just like the shriek of a panther.

"Move slowly behind me," whispered Lucy, emphasizing each word. "We'll back up to the bank and gradually make our way toward the wagons."

"Wait, Lucy." Olive didn't know why, but she suddenly knew this was no panther. Could it be the faint shuffling noises she heard? A panther moved soundlessly. Even more, Olive had long ago learned to trust her shivers. Whenever danger threatened, she could feel a prickle move up her spine until it raised goose flesh. Earlier she had felt that prickle of fear when she imagined the panther crouching on a branch. Now she felt nothing.

"Olive's right." Susan's whisper was so low they could barely make out the words. She continued more loudly, "We must stay and fight, girls. Grab a stick. Our fathers are still at the campfire and would never hear us. And even if the big boys were around, they would be stiff with fear."

"Let's go, Lucy. Please." Mary Ann's thin voice quivered.

Olive soundlessly pulled her little sister's face close enough to her own so that Mary Ann could see Olive wink in the darkness. Mary Ann didn't understand what was happening, but she understood their longtime signal—the wink meant she could trust Olive and she must play along. Her stiff shoulders seemed to relax some.

"No, Mary Ann," Lucy said, raising her voice. "We need to stand our ground. Four girls can take a panther—I just know it. And we have a duty to save Lorenzo, Charles, J. S., and the other boys. They may look big and strong, but this panther would positively terrify them if they happened upon it."

"True enough," Olive said. "If the boys came onto a panther they'd likely burst into big sobbing tears and the shame of it would follow them the rest of their lives."

A rustling of brush nearby alerted the girls. "Sobbing tears, sister?" Lorenzo burst onto the bank nearby with three indignant friends in tow. "Take that back!"

The girls started to laugh.

"The joke is on you, boys," Lucy said. "You tried to frighten us and ended up listening in on our private conversation. You know what Ma says, Lorenzo, 'eavesdroppers rarely hear well of themselves.'"

Lorenzo started laughing. He understood that the boys had been bested at their own game.

"You knew it was us all the time and were just teasing, right?" Charles Metteer did not sound convinced.

"You'll never know, now will you?" Susan flicked her hair to the back of her shoulders and laughed as the girls began walking back to camp.

As they got closer to the wagons, Olive could hear her father's agitated voice.

"I've had more than enough of his high-handedness and his strange religious beliefs." Pa rarely got angry, but Olive could tell this had been building for a long time.

"You are not the only one concerned." The voice was that of Susan's father. "The Wilders and the Kellys are concerned as well."

"It looks as if we shall have to break up this company if we mean to stay the course. Brewster seems dead set on this new plan of his. It concerns me greatly." Father paused. "He spent a year convincing us that California was to be our Promised Land. If he could change his mind that quickly over what he held to be divine direction, how can we trust him with our lives?"

Only a week out of Independence and trouble was brewing.

•   •   •

The days fell into a routine of sorts. Just as the sun began to lighten the sky, the pioneers prepared to move out. Lorenzo, always eager to start the day, stirred the embers of the fire and added just enough wood to coax it back to life. He filled water barrels while Ma boiled coffee and nursed the baby. Royce milked the cow, skimming the cream for the butter churn. Olive and Lucy helped mother prepare breakfast—cornmeal boiled with milk. Mary Ann looked after Charity Ann and the baby. Pa busied himself with hitching up the team and loading the wagon. The Oatmans managed to bolt down their breakfast while finishing preparations for the day's journey. Any leftover cornmeal mush stayed in the pan to set up. It would be sliced into cold wedges and added to dinner.

Olive felt like morning was push, push, push, and rush, rush, rush. When Mr. Brewster finally cracked his whip and yelled, "Wagons ho," harnesses clanked, oxen bellowed, wagons creaked, and wheels squeaked. When they had talked about the journey way back in Illinois, Olive pictured them flying across the prairie. If anything, the pace grew slower each day. When they came to a water crossing, the team would be unhitched and the men would attach ropes to the wagon, lower it down the bank, pull it across the river or stream, and haul it back up the far bank. The animals would then be led across and hitched back to the wagon. While the men repeated this with each wagon, the women and big girls would help the little ones across farther upstream. Charity Ann loved Olive's piggyback rides and would squeal with delight when Olive teased her with the threat of a dunking. This late in the season the water usually came up only to Olive's waist, but the few times they crossed deeper water, Pa and Lorenzo helped them across on horseback.

At the end of the first week, they came to a place called Council Grove. The wagon train had covered only about 100 miles. Early on the company had decided to halt on Saturdays to prepare for Sabbath observance on Sunday and not start again until Monday, but with rumblings of discord, the party decided to hunker down for a week and work out their differences. So after a long day, the travelers circled the wagons and set up tents, preparing to camp at Council Grove. Despite the now constant bickering, they planned for a Sunday service.

As soon as night fell, Olive crawled inside the wagon, wedging herself between her little sisters. She could hear her parents talking softly outside. Her mother no longer trusted Mr.

Brewster and seemed to think that his ideas became stranger with each day of the journey.

Pa seemed uncertain and worried. "We trusted ourselves to this train, Mary Ann. How can we break off now? Who will guide us?"

"But, Royce, we signed on to go to California. Mr. Brewster seems to change the destination every day. Every time he reads his Bible and gets out those stones, he seems to want to change directions. I feel no confidence in the man and his odd ideas."

"We have everything tied up in this venture. We do not have enough provisions to wait for another train. Besides, it is too late in the season for the Oregon Trail, and I doubt there will be any further trains planning to take the Cooke-Kearney route this year. Mary Ann, if we break off now, who will guide us?"

Who indeed? Olive worried about that more and more these days. With so much disagreement, she felt as though they were pushing forward without even knowing where they headed for sure.

After a long silence Ma asked, "What about turning back, Royce?"

"It would take every penny we have to go back, and when we got there, what would we live on? We sold our place." He sighed deeply enough for Olive to hear. "There is no turning back, only forward."

Olive finally felt herself drifting asleep to the murmuring

sounds of her parents, as she longed for her home back in Illinois.

With dawn came the first Sunday on the trail. It felt good to know that they wouldn't have to bolt from bed and begin preparations to move out. In fact, Olive remembered, they would camp here for the better part of the week.

As they gathered after breakfast to sing hymns of praise, Olive felt her lungs expand to take in the whole of God's creation. James Brewster stood up to sermonize, but Olive concentrated instead on the vastness of God. Ma didn't trust Mr. Brewster any longer. As Olive looked past their leader to the west, she saw the plain stretching on forever, dotted with oak, hickory, walnut, and butternut trees. Flowering shrubs and wildflowers of every kind followed the winding creek. The grasses stood tall, and, as a breeze blew, it created waves of movement across the grass. Olive could almost imagine they were on an ocean voyage.

As the waves rolled across the prairie again, she saw a massive outcropping of granite near the creek. Rock. It reminded her of the psalm she had memorized back in Illinois: *"The LORD is my rock, and my fortress, and my deliverer; my God, my strength, in whom I will trust . . ."*

Yes, thought Olive. *That is who will guide us. Even if Mr. Brewster turns out to be untrustworthy, God will deliver us.* She kept turning the thought around in her head. She had never really thought about it in that way before. The more she thought about it, the more the worry that marked this journey seemed to lift.

They stayed at Council Grove for the entire week. Olive, Lucy, Susan, and Mary Ann found much to do, including riding ponies across the prairies, weaving wildflowers into wreaths, and playing hide and seek in the tall grass.

Over the course of the week tempers calmed and the sense of adventure returned. As the time came to resume the journey, a renewed feeling of camaraderie seemed to settle over the company.

With the cry of "Wagons ho," they headed due west toward the Big Bend of the Arkansas River and Indian Territory.

4

Trouble on the Horizon

Indians. Although the emigrants still saw no trace of Indians, the anticipation of meeting them monopolized the travelers' thoughts. Day and night guards were posted to watch the livestock, since the inhabitants of the Indian Territories seemed to think that livestock entering their lands was fair game.

Olive wondered when they would see their first Indian. She didn't know what to expect. If one were to believe even half the stories that circulated, a person would never dare set foot in the Indian Territory. Some travelers in their company considered the Indians savages—lumping all the different tribes together; others, including her father, considered them a noble race—misunderstood, but not much different from those in the wagon train.

Sometimes at night Olive heard the hoot of an owl or the call of a coyote and recalled the boys' mimicking of a panther cry. Could those sounds actually be the call of an Indian? Olive wished she knew more about these natives and wondered if they were the heroic figures her father thought or the cruel savages others in their company thought. She guessed the truth might lie somewhere in between.

Olive usually joined Susan and Lucy as they walked. Most days the girls ran far ahead, so they could find a place to pick flowers, share secrets, laugh, and try to startle the older boys as they approached with the horses. Once Susan jumped out from behind a rock in front of J. S., and, instead of alarming him, she startled the horses and they bolted. It took the boys all afternoon to round them up and settle them down. Susan's parents made her formally apologize to the boys.

Sometimes Susan and Lucy told each other so many secrets that Olive felt like an outsider. She knew they didn't intend to ignore her, but much of their time was taken up in discussing what they referred to as "possible beaus."

During extended beau discussions, Olive stayed close to her mother or gathered the smaller children into games along the trail. As they moved deeper into Indian Territory, parents insisted the children stick close by.

On one of those days Olive walked alongside as her mother sat inside the wagon, holding the reins loosely in one hand and the baby in the other. Ma rarely sat on the seat since she preferred to sit under the canvas. A lady always tried to protect her complexion from the damaging sun. Olive loved talking to her mother, and, on the trail, time for talking was plentiful.

"Olive!" Mary Ann's voice carried from the grove up ahead along with the younger boys' version of Indian war whoops. "Help me!"

Mother sighed. "Will you see what those children are up to now, Olive?"

Olive crossed behind the wagon and ran over to the trees. The boys had tied Mary Ann to a sapling and danced around her, flailing the air and hitting the ground with sticks.

"All right boys," Olive said. "Untie Mary Ann."

"She's our captive," Royce said without missing a step. "You have to pay us a ransom for her."

"A ransom? Where did you ever hear about a ransom, young man?"

"That pam-plit of Mr. Brinshall's showed white men giving Indians beads and things to pay ransom for a captive."

"Pam-plit?" Olive couldn't figure out what he was saying. "Oh, you mean pamphlet."

"Yup. Indians don't give back prisoners without a ransom."

Olive reached down and picked up some small stones. "Here. Now let Mary Ann go. Can't you see she's getting upset?"

"Not for rocks, Olive." Royce was clearly upset. "That's not fair. That's not the way it works."

"OK." Olive decided to be creative so as not to entirely spoil their game. "Even better than a ransom is a substitution, you know."

"A substitution?" Royce was interested.

"Yes. The very best ransom of all is when someone more important than the captive offers her life in exchange."

"Is that for real, Olive?"

"Do you remember our history lesson back in Illinois about Captain John Smith of Jamestown colony?"

"I think so."

"Chief Powhatan held Captain Smith captive, and his life was only spared when Powhatan's daughter Pocahontas pleaded for his life and offered to take his place." Olive paused. "I may not be a chief's daughter, but I am older than Mary Ann and can do more things. That makes me more valuable as a prisoner. Will you take me captive and free Mary Ann?"

Royce gathered the other boys together as Mary Ann grew ever more antsy. "We agree with your trade," he finally announced. "Braves, cut down the captive and let her go free."

Two boys untied Mary Ann while two more took Olive by her arms and led her to another tree. Mary Ann ran off toward the wagon train, yelling, "I'm going to tell Ma, Royce."

As the boys tied Olive's hands behind the tree, she felt a moment of unreasonable panic. Telltale shivers ran across her shoulders, and her scalp got tight, raising the hairs on her head. *What a silly reaction to a little boy's game,* she told herself. *What's wrong with you, Olive Ann Oatman?*

As soon as they finished tying her and began their dance once more, Olive worked her hands loose and, dropping the twine, ran through their circle toward the wagons.

"Come back, Olive," Royce yelled. "You're our captive fair and square."

"But if the captive outsmarts the braves and escapes, she's free!"

"No fair!" Royce yelled as he and the boys came running after her.

The wagons had circled for the noon meal, and Olive's escape was soon forgotten in the preparations for dinner. One of the men had shot and dressed a deer the day before, so today's meal would be one of plenty. The smell of venison roasting on a makeshift spit was enough to interest any number of hungry boys.

For some reason, though, Olive could not shake her uneasy feeling. She hoped that a good meal would help restore her carefree disposition.

By the time Olive finally sat down with a plate of food, however, most of the adults had lost interest in food. Another disagreement had been brewing all morning, and in the heat of midday it had burst into a full-blown argument.

Mr. Brewster paced angrily through the camp. "You pioneers signed on under my leadership and my authority," he began.

"We certainly did not sign on to a dictatorship," Mr. Thompson replied, getting close to Mr. Brewster and punctuating certain words with a jab of his finger. "We paid you to guide us, not to bully us."

"Your strange views make us more uncomfortable with

each mile, sir," Pa said quietly. "You continue to change your mind and insist that new revelations are leading you in entirely new directions. We all agreed to go to California."

"You simply refuse to acknowledge a true prophet." Brewster's anger reached a new pitch. "If you are not open to the leading of a visionary, then I . . . I . . . ." Without finishing his sentence, he stomped off into the trees by the water.

Those left seemed stunned and busied themselves with helping children and tidying up after the meal, including the men. Olive wondered what they would do if the party split as Brewster threatened. Likely, the Lanes, the Thompsons, the Metteers and the Wilders would stay the original course with the Oatmans, taking the southern Cooke-Kearney route at the Forks. If Mr. Lane was in charge, Olive knew they would do well. He was a kind, thoughtful man who listened well and spoke carefully, but he could also make a decision and follow through.

Olive loved Pa. He was the best father and the kindest man, but how he hated to have to take a stand. This discord with Mr. Brewster affected him deeply. His back ached as badly as it had in Illinois, and he seemed nervous and jumpy. He had longed to make the trip west—to "see the elephant" as he now often described it—but Olive knew he detested trouble.

The company reached the Arkansas River at last and circled the wagons on the far bank, near Great Bend. The next day was Sunday, so when morning dawned, instead of harnessing the wagons and moving out, everyone gathered for a church service. As the group began to sing their first hymn, an eerie, discordant melody broke through. One by one the singers dropped out until only the strange whooping wails remained.

"Look," Lorenzo said, pointing to a hickory grove nearby. A band of Comanche danced around a herd of beautiful American horses and mules, some still saddled. Mr. Metteer, who had been guarding the livestock, stood very near the grove. As he edged closer to the wagons, one Comanche stepped out from behind a tree and leveled a gun at him. Mr. Metteer took a running dive and made it to camp just as the man stepped into the open, lowered his gun and made gestures of friendship.

Olive watched Pa exhale.

"Just as I thought," said Pa. "They are harmless. Seeing we mean them no harm, they offer friendship."

Pa, along with the other men, invited the Comanche into the camp. Lorenzo and some of the older boys hung back, plainly distrustful. Olive watched Lorenzo's face. Since the beginning of the journey he had seemed more like one of the men than one of the boys. She respected his instinct.

After some visiting and gesturing, with not a little bit of poking into wagons and checking out provisions, the small tribe of Comanche pulled apart and began whispering among themselves. As Lorenzo and his friends saw this, they took their weapons and crouched down alongside the wagons, just in case.

The Comanche, as if on command, dropped to one knee

and fitted arrows into their bows. Too late, the pioneers realized they'd been foolish. They had appeared weak when they invited the strangers into their circle of safety. But before a single arrow could be shot, the boys stepped into view with their loaded guns, surprising both the Comanche and their own fellow travelers.

Lowering their bows, the Comanche stood and boldly asked to be given a cow for beef. The travelers refused and the Indians reluctantly left. From that point in the journey, the guard on the livestock was doubled and the company became more wary.

The next day they crossed the river and met a government train returning from the fort. The officers reported that the livestock being driven by the Comanche had been stolen from another wagon train on their way to the fort. Those emigrants had been left stranded without their livestock.

That night Lucy and Olive both climbed into the crowded wagon to sleep. "Do you think all Indians are thieves?" asked Lucy.

"No." Olive wasn't sure why she knew that, but she did. "I wonder if the Indians think all white people are weak and foolish?"

"It looks like we don't trust them and they don't trust us, doesn't it?" Lucy sighed. "They probably don't like us coming into their land."

"Sometimes I'm just like Pa," Olive said. "I wish everyone could be friends."

"Do you ever wish we could go home, Olive?"

"Sometimes."

"Me too."

The sound of a lone wolf calling across the prairie ended the conversation. Olive tried to keep an adventurous spirit, but tonight she felt insignificant and misplaced. A small sad cough coming from the direction of Lucy reminded her that at least she was not alone.

• • •

The next day the wagon train crossed the Arkansas River. It took all day. As the Oatman wagon made its way across the river it tipped slightly, dumping a few things into the river: a mixing bowl, Charity Ann's boots, and two oilcloth sacks—one containing the Bible and the other the lilac cutting.

"Lorenzo! Royce!" Ma called out. "Please catch those things before they are carried away."

Lorenzo and Pa had to get the wagon across the river before they could retrieve the belongings. The Bible, the bowl, and one of Charity Ann's boots were caught in a tangle of branches downstream. They eventually found the other boot on the opposite bank, wedged between two stones. The lilac pouch could not be found.

"I cannot believe I've lost the chance of continuing the Sperry lilac in California." Mother searched the banks for the remaining oilcloth sack.

All the wagons finally crossed, and Mr. Brewster gave the

call to move out. Olive understood her mother's sense of loss and hung back slightly. Now that the company traveled deep within Indian Territory they needed to stay close to the wagons, but she hated to give up, for her mother's sake.

As the last wagon rolled across the grass, Olive tried one more clump of rushes. There, wedged between the stalks, lay the oilcloth sack. *Thank You, God.*

"Olive," her mother called from the wagon. "Don't linger, it's too dangerous."

Olive didn't need to linger. "I found it, Ma! I found the lilac cutting." She ran toward the wagon, waving the bag in the air.

"Oh, Olive!" Her mother burst into tears. "I don't know what's wrong with me. It shouldn't mean so much." She took the pouch from Olive, kissing her daughter's fingers. "Thank you. Sometimes it feels as if there's just been too much loss."

• • •

The feeling of loss continued. When the company reached the Santa Fe Pass, at a place called The Forks, the discord erupted, and the troubled Brewster party finally decided to part ways. Mr. Brewster and about half the others decided to abandon the journey and settle near Santa Fe. Olive's family along with Mr. and Mrs. Lane, the Thompsons, the Wilders, and others headed down into Mexican Territory toward the town of Socorro. In some ways the split was a relief, especially since it ended the constant bickering. The smaller party respected each other and looked forward to a peaceful crossing.

As the journey continued, the grass grew drier, the dust thicker, the air hotter, and water more scarce. The sun burned down on them during midday, and the nighttime temperatures grew cold.

As Olive and Lucy walked alongside the wagon, they watched Mr. Lane coaxing the lead wagon along. "I don't know what we'd do without Mr. Lane," Olive said. "Doesn't he somehow seem to be the father of our whole group?"

"I've thought the same thing," Lucy said. "He's wise, he's kind, and he seems to keep us going."

The country grew more mountainous. The steep inclines and descents took their toll. Most days they only traveled about a fourth of the distance they had covered on the prairies. Somehow the sense of adventure disappeared.

Just a few days past the Rio Grande, Mr. Lane took sick. Pa said he thought it must be the mountain fever. Everyone in the party waited and hoped, but in a short time, Mr. Lane died.

With heavy hearts, the travelers buried him at the foot of a hill. Olive, Susan, and Lucy dug up small flowering shrubs and planted a mass of color on his grave. That day marked the saddest day of the trip so far. No one talked—it felt as if their father had died and they were all orphans.

It can't get much worse than this, Olive thought as she scuffed her way alongside the wagon. *Who will take care of us now?* She looked over at Pa and saw the hunch of his shoulders. *Yes. There's no way it can get worse than—*

A shiver crawled along Olive's shoulders. *What?* She turned around to focus on the dusty back trail just in time to watch a group of Apaches turn their horses off the path and splash down into the stream.

Maybe it can get worse.

5

The Gila Trail

Winter settled on the land, but still no rain. How strange to be so cold and yet so thirsty at the same time. It wasn't like any winter Olive had experienced. After one long day without water, the wagons finally circled, and the travelers bedded down without having found a single creek, spring, or pool. The oxen bawled all night long. Babies whimpered and mothers worried. Olive could feel her lips cracking and her tongue getting thick and sticky from thirst. Her mouth gave a cracking, smacking sound every time she opened it.

By morning the air had turned frigid, and snow had fallen during the night, capping all the mountains around the thirsty travelers. What a cruel joke to be looking at snow on the mountains while dying of thirst in the valley.

They decided not to even bother cooking breakfast. Without water there could be neither corn mush nor coffee and, as thirsty as they were, dry food could never be coaxed down swollen throats. Besides, rations were so short that each person received less than a handful of food for a whole day. Their only hope was in pressing on toward possible water.

Getting the thirsty oxen hitched and moving took real patience. Pa took solace in knowing that oxen were best suited to go long distances without water. Had they used only horses, they would have been stranded here.

By midmorning hope began to flicker on the horizon. Up ahead, the tired, thirsty, hungry pioneers could see what looked like a stand of timber. Timber like that could only grow near water. At first they hardly dared to hope. They had seen many mirages in the desert—places that looked like lakes and trees but disappeared into the haze as they drew near. These trees, however, did not disappear as they drove toward them.

After a full day's travel they reached the grove of trees. A creek ran through the woodland, and though the water was too cold to drink in any quantity, plenty of wood lay around for the gathering. The chill was taken off the frigid water over a hastily built fire, and everyone drank deep and long.

Not only did they find water, but wild game was plentiful as well. As soon as the wagons had been circled and the area secured, the men set out to hunt. They found turkey, deer, antelope, and wild sheep. To the half-starved travelers, it seemed as if a feast had been laid before them. They decided to stay for the better part of a week, gathering strength and letting their livestock fatten up on the rich grasses. The women began drying meat over smoky fires for the journey. The children picked the few fall berries that still clung to bushes.

Susan took out her violin once again in the evenings, and the emigrants enjoyed singing. Olive could feel the group drawing closer once again. Her own family seemed to regain their sense of adventure.

"Olive," Royce called holding up three turkey feathers. "Want to play Indian brave and Indian squaw with me?"

"I don't think those are good words, Royce." Olive noticed that the Indians they met never used those words at all.

"What words?"

"Squaw and brave."

"What do you call them?"

"We say 'Indian' because that's what they were called by mistake when the very first explorers came to this country. Pa says they never call themselves Indians. They use only their tribe names, like 'I am Walapai' or 'I am Pima.'"

"Not Indian?" Royce was confused.

"No. Pa says their names for themselves usually mean 'the people.'" Olive had been thinking about this. If the Oatmans were going to be living near Indians, she wanted to know more about them to lessen the fear she too often felt.

"So what do you call a squaw?"

"I don't know, Royce." Olive wondered if one just said "Apache woman." She heard Indians referred to all different ways, many of them cruel. "Too bad we just didn't learn their names so we could call them by name like we do Mr. Metteer or Mrs. Thompson."

"Well, do you want to play Indians or not?"

"Sure. My legs could use a little running. I don't want to grow soft during our rest." She stuck a turkey feather in her hair and ran round and round with Royce. How good it felt to be playing with her exuberant little brother.

• • •

One of the worries of the last few days had been Mary Ann. She continued to rest but did not seem to be bouncing back as the others did. She'd developed a cough that worried Ma.

While Lucy walked with Susan—Olive suspected they were looking for berries to stain their lips—Olive stayed near Mary Ann.

"Olive, tell me a story," said Mary Ann.

"What story do you want to hear?"

"Oh dear, how about *Beauty and the Beast*?"

"How did I know you'd choose that one, little sister?" Olive laughed. "That was always your favorite one from our book of fairy tales." She helped Mary Ann settle into the quilts propped up against an outcropping of rock.

"I hope I can remember how this goes . . ." Olive said with a smile.

"I'll help if you forget."

"Once upon a time there lived a rich merchant who had . . . let's see, four daughters."

"Four?" interrupted Mary Ann, "I thought it was two."

"Who's telling this story? You or me?" Olive gave Mary

Ann that broad wink that meant "play along with me."

"All right, Olive, but make it really good."

"All the girls were pretty. The oldest, Lucy, was golden; the next daughter, Olive, was raven; the baby, Charity Ann, was a cherub; but it was Mary Ann who was accounted the real beauty. In fact, they no longer called her Mary Ann, they just called her Beauty."

At this, Mary Ann blushed and made an embarrassed *tsk* sound while she pretended to thump Olive on the leg, but she didn't interrupt again.

"Unfortunately the sisters were vain, especially Lucy who squeezed berry juice on her lips to deepen their color when nobody was looking." Olive looked over toward the creek where Susan and Lucy sat talking. "The girls' jealousy of Beauty grew deeper with each passing day as they saw their own vanity contrasted by her modesty and charm. Beauty knew contentment and peace and longed to stay forever with her father in their safe and comfortable home. Bad financial troubles hit, though, and his business failed without warning. The family lost their home and their business and ended up penniless."

"That's like us, isn't it, Olive?"

"I guess so," Olive replied, thinking back to LaHarpe and the mercantile. "Beauty's pa decided to venture out, seeking to regain his wealth. Lucy, Olive, and Charity Ann didn't care a fig about the troubles. They only knew they were tired of being poor. When Pa, who longed to give his daughters the finest, asked them what he should bring them, the sisters demanded he bring them expensive garments. Each one dreamed up an elaborate and expensive dress. When Pa turned to Beauty, she thought for minute and asked for a fragrant lilac bloom."

"Oh dear, I do like lilacs, Olive."

"A long time passed and, sadly, Beauty's pa failed in his tries to regain his wealth. He finally gave up and began to make his way home through the forest when he found himself trapped in a snowstorm. Just when he could go no farther he stumbled on a seemingly deserted palace."

"Was it beautiful?"

"Well, it felt warm, and the table was set with delicious food. After eating his fill, he found a bed all made up with fresh linens. He sank into the featherbed without having seen a single living soul. The next morning he woke to the scent of lilacs blooming in the garden. Without even dressing, he walked into the garden where he saw the perfect lilac bloom for Beauty. Using the golden shears which lay alongside, he snipped that fragrant lilac."

"Oh dear, I know what happens next, Olive. A hideous beast appears out of nowhere and says that for his theft of the lilac he must die."

Olive paused. "Do you want to hear the rest?"

"Please, Olive, don't stop."

"Thinking of his daughters, the father begged for his life. The beast listened to his pleas and finally agreed to let him go free if one of his daughters would come back to take his place, paying ransom with her own life. If she refused, then Pa must return to die himself. The beast gave him a chest filled with gold and jewels and sent him home. The treasure allowed the father to buy his daughters as many pretty dresses and bonnets as they wanted."

"Did Beauty get bonnets?" Mary Ann asked.

"Don't you remember? Beauty gets the lilac bloom. As Pa handed Beauty the lilac, he couldn't help but tell her what happened. Beauty—being as good as she was beautiful—insisted on taking her father's place, and so she returned with him to the beast's home where he reluctantly left her."

"The palace?"

"Yes, I meant the beast's palace." Olive continued, "At first the beast frightened Beauty and she avoided looking at him, but he treated her well. He gave her beautiful gowns and sweets and things she'd never ask for. Every evening he visited her at suppertime. A friendship slowly grew, and Beauty looked forward to her visits with the beast. At the end of each visit the beast respectfully asked Beauty to be his wife. She politely refused, though she promised never to leave the palace."

"Oh dear, she can't marry the beast can she, Olive?" Mary Ann asked. "He scares her, doesn't he?"

"What do you think?"

"Maybe she's getting used to him?"

"Maybe. But one day Beauty looked into a mirror and saw

a faint image of her father, growing weak with worry over her. He desperately missed her and she him. Beauty's eyes were still red from crying when the beast came for their evening visit. When he asked if anything was the matter, she begged leave to pay a visit to her father. The beast laid his head on the table for a long minute but agreed on the condition that she return in seven days. He told her if she tarried, he would die."

"Would he really?"

"I don't know. She believed him, though." Olive continued, "The next morning Beauty woke up at home in her old bed. Pa was overjoyed to see her."

"What about the sisters?"

"Unfortunately the sisters stomped around, again jealous of Beauty. Especially since she seemed content and had even more bonnets and dresses than they did. When she told them about the palace, it sounded so rich and luxurious that they decided to keep her away from the beast. Each day they talked Beauty into staying just one day longer. Believing that her sisters finally loved her, she couldn't bear to leave. On the tenth night, however, she dreamed of the beast and saw him dying."

"He's really dying?"

"Yes. Beauty closed her eyes tight and wished herself back with the beast. When she opened her eyes, she found herself back in the palace, standing over the beast as he lay dying of a broken heart. Almost too late, she realized that she loved and respected the beast. As his eyes started to close for the last time, Beauty put her hand on his cheek and whispered that she would be honored to marry him. With those words, the beast turned into a prince. Her father and sisters eventually joined her at the palace for the wedding, and they all lived happily ever after."

"I thought the sisters were turned into statues until they said sorry for their faults and begged Beauty's forgiveness?"

"Well, who's telling this story, Beauty?"

Mary Ann laughed and seemed to be in a happier mood than Olive had seen her for a long time.

• • •

As the small wagon train resumed their journey after a week's rest, Olive wished she felt as cheered as Mary Ann. The gnawing hunger was gone, each family had filled all their water barrels, dried meat had been packed down in smaller barrels, and the animals were well rested. Olive couldn't understand why she felt so uneasy.

As they traveled deeper into Mexico, Olive couldn't help watching the back trail. Ever since their trail had turned south, sightings of Indians had grown more frequent. Most groups seemed as interested in the emigrants as the emigrants were in the Indians. Sometimes Pa spoke to them in Spanish. Sometimes they spoke back in a halting mixture of Spanish, English, and sign. The travelers were in Apache country, but it seemed that few of the Indian groups they saw came from the same tribe. Olive began to realize there were many different tribes even within those they called the

Apache.

Some Indian tribes seemed to be traveling to trade with the Apache. One tribe, who called themselves the Havasupai, had what they called *hishi*—strands of glass beads that they used for trade. It seemed that they traded *hishi* for blankets, furs, and even salt.

The more Olive watched the Indians, or talked to those who knew them, the more she saw the differences.

The Indians who worried Olive most were bands of young men who sometimes trailed the wagon train. They seemed to take pride in outdoing each other by doing foolish things. Sometimes they reminded Olive of the wild young men who had lived near them in Illinois but hung around taverns, talking loudly, fighting, and always challenging each other.

One group of Yavapai in particular seemed troublesome. They spoke broken Spanish and often trailed the wagon train, making Olive wonder if they were outcasts of some sort. Didn't they have families? As she watched for their trail, she noticed they rode shod horses. Indians did not put metal horseshoes on their ponies, so this meant that the horses these Yavapai rode were most likely stolen.

One moonless night, after a daytime visit by a band of young Indian men, the dogs began barking and continued till almost morning. Their behavior was so unusual—barking and running back to the wagons, going out to bark again—that the men stayed up the whole night through. They sat or kneeled near the wagons with guns ready to shoot. Other than the dogs, however, they never heard another movement or sound.

When the sun rose, they saw crisscrossing tracks of men and horses all around their circled wagons. Twenty head of livestock came up missing. Somehow, the Indians had silently driven them away in the dark right under the watch of the men. Some of the animals belonged to the teams, making it impossible to continue as before. Each family made the hard decision to lighten their loads. This meant leaving some of their heavier belongings along the side of the trail.

As the now smaller teams pulled the wagons away from their campsite, Olive couldn't keep from looking at the stack of treasures left behind. Seeing Ma's beloved stoneware crock sitting crookedly atop the pile made Olive's throat hurt until she could no longer swallow her tears.

6

The Shadow of Death

The trail that stretched out ahead of them seemed endless. When they set out from Independence, a sense of adventure and anticipation had colored each mile. While Olive walked beside the wagon now, California seemed like a cruel hoax.

"Olive?" Her mother rode in the front of the wagon. "Are you feeling well?"

"Yes."

"This trail beats down even the brightest disposition, doesn't it?"

"I'm sorry, Ma. I don't wish to be a worry for you. Just like our numbers have diminished mile by mile, I feel as if I am drying up with each footstep—I am diminishing as well."

"I understand, Olive Ann. We never anticipated the hardship of this journey and find ourselves ill-prepared." Her mother did not ordinarily confide in Olive, but the deeper into the journey they went, the more distant Pa became. "Your father blames himself for misjudging the difficulty, and the regret sits hard on his shoulders."

"I know. I've watched his nervousness return."

"You've always been so observant, Olive." Ma reached out her hand to touch Olive's cheek. "The one thing that hasn't changed is God's care on our journey. I sense Him closer than ever."

"Do you really think so, Ma?" Olive paused. "If God is close, why have we suffered so much? Why didn't He help us resolve our differences with Mr. Brewster so we could stay together? Why did He let Mary Ann weaken? Why couldn't He safeguard our animals?"

"Oh, Olive, I don't know the answer to those questions."

"I don't mean to be disrespectful, but I feel alone— terribly alone."

"We are not alone, Olive. I sense that strongly." Ma reached back into the wagon and drew out the oilcloth sack with the Bible. She opened the flap and took out the book and thumbed through the pages. "Do you remember this psalm you memorized back in Illinois? 'The LORD is my rock, and my fortress, and my deliverer; my God, my strength, in whom I will trust. . . . The sorrows of death compassed me, and the floods of ungodly men made me afraid. . . . In my distress I called upon the LORD. . . . He delivered me from my strong enemy, and from them which hated me: for they were too strong for me. . . . He brought me forth also into a large place; he delivered me, because he delighted in me.'"

"I remember. The passage comes from Psalm 18." Olive loved those parts of the psalm.

"As we travel through this territory and see the anger of the Apaches, I see them as our strong enemy. I sometimes think that ungodly men grieve the Lord as surely as they grieve us." Ma seemed to be working some of this out as she talked to Olive. "Perhaps as He walks alongside us and sees our trouble and discouragement, He weeps with us."

"I guess I never thought about Him walking with us, step by step. I wish He'd just make everything better."

"Yes." Ma laughed. "Wouldn't it be easy if the Lord just whisked us out of every tight spot we ever wedged ourselves in?"

The wagon creaked as the wheels inched along the dry, packed ground. Olive continued to walk alongside.

"You know what I think, Olive?" Ma asked after a long time. "I think God understands that we only grow as we walk through the trouble we get ourselves in, one step at a time."

Olive didn't answer. It might be true, but she liked the fairy tales better—like *Beauty and the Beast*, where all Beauty had to do was wish herself in a different place and it happened.

Ma had it right about the increasing anger of the Apaches. The travelers stopped in the Mexican village of Tubac, hoping to buy more provisions. The people could offer nothing for sale, and they told how the Apaches destroyed every field they planted. Did the Apaches resent strangers encroaching on their territory?

After leaving Tubac, they traveled along the Santa Cruz River, where the grasses again grew lush and the land bloomed. Those Mexicans living in the settlement of Santa Cruz tried to talk the travelers into staying. They explained that the Apaches respected the American rifles far more than the weapons of the Mexican farmers. The travelers pressed on despite the welcome.

Eighty miles farther, it was the town of Tucson that tempted several in the party. Because food and provisions were plentiful, the travelers stayed nearly a month. Olive could often hear the men discussing the journey.

"Oatman, it's foolish to press on. Our numbers are too small to offer us any safety," Mr. Metteer said.

"The Mexicans here in Tucson welcome us to stay and work with them," Mr. Brinshall added.

"We've come so far. Do we truly want to stay here where the Apaches seem to be waging a battle, when we can press on and reach the safety of California?" Pa could not let go of his dream.

"But safety is in numbers—numbers we no longer possess. I think we should stay here until we can connect with other emigrants." Mr. Thompson hated arguing. Olive saw that it took resolve for him to stick to his judgment.

The discussions continued. When the wagons finally pulled out of Tucson, only three families made up the train— the Oatmans, the Wilders, and the Kellys. How wrenching it was to say good-bye to friends. No one would be missed as much as Susan.

When Susan first drew Lucy and Olive apart to tell them, the girls couldn't believe they would really be separated. They had spent the last six months together—eating, sleeping, playing, and dreaming together. How do you say goodbye to someone who'd become as close as a sister?

"We won't say good-bye," Lucy said. The three girls were sitting on an old adobe half wall in the village of Tucson.

"Are you going to stay with me?" Susan was confused.

"No. We cannot stay. Our father is determined to make it to California." Lucy spoke those words with resignation. She knew he would not change his mind. "I meant that we mustn't say the word 'good-bye.'"

"I hate farewells." Olive kicked the wall with her heels. She'd had to say good-bye to friends in LaHarpe and then to friends in Fulton.

"What do we say?" Susan asked.

"How about 'Race you to California!'" Lucy laughed, and the other two joined in. The journey west seemed to drag on forever. The idea of a race was too funny to even contemplate.

"Let's just say, 'Until California,'" Olive suggested.

They agreed and then tried not to think about the separation. As the days drew near, Olive almost wished to hurry the leave-taking. Dragging out the good-byes made them harder than ever.

As they pulled out, the Oatman wagon left last. Olive and

Lucy walked backward looking back toward Tucson until Susan was no more than a speck on the horizon.

Olive's calves hurt from walking backward. She decided that she'd ride in the wagon for a while despite the bumps and jostles. If God was walking alongside, she wondered if He missed the others as much as she did.

• • •

Pa wasn't the only one becoming increasingly nervous. The constant tension wore on everyone's nerves. With only three wagons they couldn't even circle the wagons at night for safety. Having only three men to take turns guarding livestock and manning night watch meant that no one slept much.

By the time they reached the Indian Pima villages it was February 18, 1851. Olive found out the date from Mrs. Wilder and scratched it on the side of the wagon. She was determined to mark time in some way.

The Pimoles had little extra to share with the visitors, but again, they begged the small group of travelers to stay and help them defend their village.

"Royce—" Mr. Wilder and Mr. Kelly came together, but Mr. Kelly did the talking. "We've decided to stay here in the safety of the village for now."

Pa did not say a word. He simply stood in front of them as if they had slapped him.

"We know you want to press on, but please consider your family. Please stay with us."

Pa walked away.

Ma, Olive, and Lucy hoped he was thinking about their words. Lorenzo seemed troubled as well and followed Pa. Olive watched her brother's face. She hoped he'd talk to Pa.

That evening a visitor came into camp. He introduced himself as Dr. Lecount. He'd been traveling to and from Fort Yuma and reported that he had seen no Indian activity whatsoever.

Pa questioned him closely and was satisfied that it was safe to travel to the Fort. So on March 11th the Oatman family set out alone along the trail to Yuma—Ma and Pa, Lorenzo, Lucy, Olive, Mary Ann, Royce, Charity Ann, and the baby. They were quiet and fearful, despite the promise of safety.

Olive, who had long ago made a habit of watching their back trail, often saw what seemed like shadowy figures on horses. One morning, a few days after starting out alone, Olive saw the footprints of shod horses near their camp. So much for Dr. Lecount's prediction of a safe, uneventful journey. She decided not to even mention it. Nothing could be done about it anyway.

From that point on, nothing but trouble hit. The teams weakened, and sometimes it was all Pa and Lorenzo could do to get them moving. Food grew scarce, and Olive's shivery feeling almost never left.

On the sixth day out of the Pima villages, Dr. Lecount and his guide passed them on their way back to Fort Yuma. Seeing the trouble they had, he told Pa he'd hurry to the fort and send help back to rescue them. This cheered Pa considerably.

That night they finally reached the Gila River. Swollen with rainwater, the crossing took much work and constant pushing and pulling of exhausted oxen. The wagon finally mired on a sand bar halfway across the river.

"Lorenzo," Pa said. "Just unhitch the livestock and let them wander. We'll stay here tonight and climb the far bank to the plateau in the morning when we are fresh."

Lorenzo did as Father asked. He kept a close watch on the back trail. He also kept a close watch on his sisters and Royce.

Olive worried when she looked at Father. He seemed to have shrunk in size and his shoulders sagged. Maybe he was just tired. Ma showed strength, and they all seemed cheered by her bustling energy. Pa gathered wood, and Olive watched the little ones. Ma and Lucy made bread and cooked supper.

The winds howled through the ravine that whole night long and nobody slept. To Olive it felt like the valley of the shadow of death. The long hours were spent talking about what they would do if an attack came.

"I'll hold 'em off until everyone gets to safety," said Royce.

"Oh dear. I'll run as fast I can," said Mary Ann as she coughed in the night air.

"All I know," said Olive, "is that I shall not be taken captive. If they captured me, I would find a way to escape."

"If any of us were taken captive, I'd not rest until I rescued them," Lorenzo said. Olive looked at her brother and recognized the steel in his words. How he had grown since leaving Illinois. And how she had come to respect him.

Morning finally came. The team, refreshed by a night of eating scant tufts of grass and drinking cool water, seemed ready to proceed. Lorenzo hitched them up, and inch by inch they began to pull the wagon out of the sand.

Progress was so slow that Pa had the children unload much of the wagon and hand carry the things to the far bank and then up the steep cliff to the plateau. Mary Ann carried only the Bible and the lilac cutting. Olive carried all the bedding, and did her best to keep it dry.

It took all morning to reach the far side of the Gila, and, by then, the much-worn animals were spent. Pa decided to rest until late afternoon before trying to entice the oxen to pull the wagon up the 200-foot cliff.

Late that afternoon they resumed the ordeal. Rocks tumbled into the river below as the oxen slipped and slid up the steep incline, pulling the almost empty wagon. The sun began to set by the time they reached the tableland of the plateau. Tired though they were, the family ate a quick supper of bread and bean soup.

"To what do we owe all these long faces?" Ma asked. "It's time to cheer up. We made it—the work of fording the Gila is behind us, and we shall have a full moon to travel by. The Indians call it the windbreak moon."

Pa did not say anything.

"We'll make some good time this night while it's cool, and we'll be at the fort before long." Ma tried to cover Pa's dejection with words of encouragement.

As the children and Pa began to repack the wagon, Lorenzo glanced down the trail they'd covered that afternoon. "Look!" Lorenzo pointed to the trail back down to the Gila. A band of young Yavapai men wearing loose wolf skins tied at the shoulder and draped across their chests came into view. They continued to walk toward the Oatman camp, leading their horses.

Olive recognized them. They were the ones who'd followed on and off for much of their journey. One glance at her father's face terrified Olive. The always cheerful, stubbornly optimistic outlook of the man who left Illinois just seven months ago had given way to stark fear.

Lorenzo saw the look as well and moved to get his gun. Olive knew he believed bluster was the best tactic. She trusted his instinct. These were not ordinary Indians like the gentle Pimoles or even the livestock-raiding Apaches. Olive had observed them long enough to know that these men were renegades and troublemakers.

Father seemed to somehow stiffen himself, making an effort to take control as he welcomed them in Spanish.

Oh, no, Pa, thought Olive. *These are not your noble Indians. Show strength. Bluff. Don't let them see a single shred of weakness.*

Too late. Pa's natural gentility and courtesy led him to offer them a peace offering of some food and a pipe-full of tobacco. The men demanded more as they boldly came into the camp and began poking into boxes and rummaging through the parcels still on the ground.

"Children," said Ma quietly. "Slowly begin loading our things back into the wagon. Mary Ann, sit on that stone over there and hold the reins of the oxen so they don't move during the packing. Olive and Lucy, move back to the far side."

As the family began to break camp, the Yavapai pulled off to the side of the camp and began a vigorous whispered debate in the Yuman tongue. The family couldn't understand the language, but they could read the agitation.

As Olive loaded one large box, shivers started across her shoulders as her hair stood on end. A moment later she heard an almost inhuman shriek, and she feared she would die at this very place.

The confusion, the dust, the screams, the cries of her family—it was all too noisy, frightening, and confusing for Olive to comprehend what was taking place. She remembered hearing a sickening thud and feeling Lucy slump down the side of the wagon onto Olive's feet. Lucy's weight nearly knocked Olive down.

She felt a roaring in her ears that jumbled all the sounds. Everything happened as if in slow motion. Olive stood in stunned paralysis and waited to die. Through a fog of dust she watched one of the men raise a club high above him and bring it down onto Lorenzo's head. Her brother hit the ground hard. She saw his eyes open, but then he squeezed them shut.

As Olive watched the frenzied attackers rummaging through the wagon, she realized they had no plans to kill her. With her whole family dead, would she have to go on alone?

Perhaps Mother had been right, and God had accompanied them on this journey—because, although Olive could not feel a thing, she somehow knew that God wept at the evil all around them.

The Captive Journey

O live, where's Mama?"

Olive thought she was hearing things. The quivery voice was almost inaudible. "Mary Ann?"

Still sitting stiffly on the rock and holding the reins of the lead ox was Mary Ann. Her face was drained, and she shook uncontrollably.

"Oh, Mary Ann." Olive wrapped arms around her sister and they sat huddled together, little caring what would happen next.

The men went through every box in the wagon. They ripped the canvas off the spines and took the wheels off as well. One man searched until he found every piece of food and tied it together in a piece of canvas and put the bundle aside. Another took his knife and ripped open the featherbed, laughing as the feathers floated around the camp.

Olive shielded Mary Ann from the scene as best she could,

81

though the little girl did not seem to comprehend anything.

After their attackers had plundered as much of their belongings as they could carry, they prodded Olive and Mary Ann to move and herded them back toward the river. Olive couldn't help looking back to see her family one last time. Not a single tear came to her eyes—it was as if she viewed a tableau. Seeing Lucy's tangled hair and crumpled form tossed in the dust of the desert gave Olive a momentary jolt of reality.

"Until California, dear sister, until California."

Discarded on the rocky ground near Ma and the baby, Olive saw the partially unwrapped oilcloth bundle with the slip from Ma's lilac bush.

And Pa, ever-hopeful Pa. Olive remembered that day back in Fulton when she heard the story of the farmer who saw the elephant. The man shrugged off the loss of his entire crop spilled in the ditch and said it was worth it to have seen the beast. *What a stupid story!*

One of her captors put his club in the middle of her back and gave a hard shove until she stumbled onto the path back down to the river. She could no longer see the remnants of her life that lay scattered on the plateau.

"Where's Mama, Olive?"

Olive looked at Mary Ann. When the family forded the river this afternoon, they had all removed their shoes. When the Yavapai had come into the camp, neither Mary Ann nor Olive had yet put on their shoes—they now found themselves barefoot and stumbling along a rocky trail. "Mama went to heaven, Mary Ann. With the baby in her arms, she went to heaven."

Mary Ann continued walking without commenting. Olive wondered how she could tell the seven-year-old that Pa had died along with their beloved Lucy, Royce, and little Charity Ann as well. Even Lorenzo, who always took care of them— gone. Maybe it didn't matter. She and Mary Ann would undoubtedly be dead before morning. Maybe her sister would never have to know.

After following the trail about a half of a mile beyond the river, they came upon the place the Yavapai must have camped the night before. Their captors stopped and prepared a meal, using some of the provisions taken from the Oatmans. Olive watched a man start a fire using a flint and some wild cotton they carried with them. The mundane act of cooking supper seemed at such odds to the events of just an hour ago. The shorter man mixed some flour with water and cooked the flat loaf of dough directly in the ash of the fire. This hard lump was then soaked in the bean soup before eating.

The Yavapai pushed some bread toward the girls, but the smell of food caused Olive's stomach to lurch. One man laughed at her refusal. Olive felt as if the captors enjoyed seeing her distress. She decided it was important to keep her grief in check.

Mary Ann showed no grief at all. Olive could tell that her sister was still in shock. She moved stiffly—almost doll-like. For now that was a blessing.

Olive remembered the whispered conversation of the night before when she and her brothers and sisters worried about an Indian attack. She had vowed to find some way to escape if taken captive. She looked over at Mary Ann, staring blankly into the night. What foolish words. She never considered that she might have someone to protect. And even if Mary Ann were not here, how did one go about escaping?

She looked up at the cliff leading up to the plateau. The journey from the Pima villages was hard enough with their whole family to help. How could she manage the escape, the journey, and still care for Mary Ann? *Besides,* she thought as she looked at the men assigned to watch them, *even if we managed to slip away from these experienced trackers, they'd have us back in no time.* It was easy enough to talk big when you're snuggled up with your brothers and sisters, but Olive realized that when she found herself on the trail with a pack of killers and a stunned little sister, it became another matter.

Snuggled up with brothers and sisters . . . Olive could not believe they were gone. Gone.

"Yakoa!"

The man angrily gestured toward the trail. Apparently they planned to move out tonight. While Olive had contemplated the impossibility of escape, her captors had packed up the campsite.

Olive took Mary Ann's hand and pulled her to her feet. The club poking into Olive's back again was the signal to walk. Five Indians seemed to be in charge of them, the rest busied themselves in moving the livestock and carrying their plunder.

The pace outstripped the strength of the sisters in a short time. They had been on the trail for months, but the Indians moved at a gallop. Even running and stumbling along, Olive and Mary Ann kept lagging behind. Their bare feet were cut and bleeding, their legs scratched and bruised, and their lungs burned with the exertion. Olive determined early not to complain about anything. She'd keep up or die trying. As best as she could figure, they were traveling about five miles each hour.

As they climbed higher, the girls were bullied and pushed along. Olive looked back at Mary Ann and saw tears silently streaming down her cheeks. If only there was something Olive could do.

"Beauty," Olive whispered to Mary Ann, winking to let her know it was a new game.

Mary Ann looked up at Olive, shaking her head as if to wake up.

"Keep climbing, Beauty. The palace cannot be far."

"Yakoa!" screamed one of the men as he raised his club.

Mary Ann sat down in the middle of the trail. "I cannot go any farther, Olive."

"Come on, please get up, Mary Ann."

"I cannot even feel my feet, Olive. I don't care if they kill me. They are bad men."

The angriest man grabbed Mary Ann and tried to put her

on her feet, but she let her body go limp and slide out of his grip. Olive's heart began thudding in her ears as he began to hit Mary Ann. Mary Ann simply did not care.

"Stop!" Olive said, getting in between the furious Yavapai and the exhausted girl. The man turned some of his blows toward Olive before another man stepped in to pick up Mary Ann. He slung her over his shoulder like a sack of flour and, without a word, started off at the same hurried pace.

Olive followed behind. She could see the blood from Mary Ann's badly cut feet dripping down the man's back.

The breakneck pace continued. Olive watched the sky and figured they traveled mostly in a northeasterly direction. To keep herself from panic, she began noting landmarks and trails. They traveled over the bluffs of a high mountain chain—it must have still been the Gila Mountains. Eventually they moved down into a winding valley.

As she watched the route, she again considered the possibility of escape. This was no game like the one Royce and his friends played back on the trail, and there was no wagon train to run back to after wriggling out of schoolboy tethers of twine.

Every time her mind wandered back to recent memories, she remembered that her family was gone—utterly and forever gone. Who even wanted to escape? She wanted to join her mother and father and family in heaven.

"Olive?"

She heard the faint whisper of Mary Ann, slumped over

the wolfskin-covered back of the Yavapai striding ahead of her.

"Don't leave me, Olive."

"I'm here, Mary Ann." Olive shook her head to clear her thoughts. They weren't all dead. She knew that she had to live as long as Mary Ann lived. For some reason the killers had spared Olive and Mary Ann. Her sister needed her.

After several hours of travel, while it was still night, they reached a flat sandy meadow in what seemed like a box canyon, rimmed by high mountains. Mary Ann was dumped onto the sand like a bundle of rags. The men seemed very familiar with the place and, for the first time, did not appear to be watching their back trail and hurrying from some hidden enemy.

The thought of an unseen rescuer had not occurred to Olive. Dr. Lecount had hurried to Fort Yuma to send back help to the Oatman party. When they came upon the campsite, would they know that two family members were missing? She thought it very likely since Dr. Lecount kept saying he'd tell the commander that a family with seven children traveled alone.

In fact, the reason Indians usually took prisoners was for ransom. The Indians learned that the army would pay handsomely for the return of captives. Once Mr. Brewster had mentioned that Apaches very often took young girls, not to make them wives, as so many silly dime novels suggested, but because they were easily captured and subdued. Mr. Brewster also said that many of the tribes had discovered that girls who were raised to be submissive gave the captors less trouble. Besides, nothing loosened the pocketbooks of Americans faster than the thought of "helpless young girls held by savages."

Olive wondered if their captors had begun to have second thoughts about how easily they could control her and her sister. As Olive pictured her frail seven-year-old sister sitting in the road, refusing to take another step, and a frustrated Yavapai throwing her over his shoulder, she smiled for the first time since the massacre. Her mother's strength had sustained their family over many a bumpy road. Perhaps these Indians would discover that they'd underestimated the pluck of an Oatman female.

They'd rested silently for about two hours when another band of Yavapai came in by a different route, herding the Oatman livestock. In the excited conversation that followed, the girls were able to huddle together tightly and whisper to each other unnoticed.

"Mama and Pa died, didn't they, Olive." It was not a question.

"Yes. And Lucy, Lorenzo, Royce, Charity Ann, and the baby."

"I know. I saw it."

"I am so glad we have each other, Mary Ann. We need to stay strong and be ready to escape or be ransomed."

"Where would we go?" Mary Ann's question made sense. Where *would* they go?

"I think we would go to Fort Yuma, and they'd give escort back to Ma's relatives in New York. Or maybe we could go to Susan's family staying in Tucson."

"Oh dear, my feet hurt."

"I know. I wish they at least waited until we had shoes and socks on." Olive realized an important thing. It was easier to talk about the present—even the present sufferings—than to think about the past.

"Remember how Ma used to say that she believed God walked with us on the journey and that He grieved for our troubles?"

"I remember. Do you think so, Olive?"

"Ma said so. I want to think about getting us out of trouble, and I'm going to let the Lord grieve for the evil that took our family."

"Can we remember the good things about our family?"

"I hope we can, Mary Ann. It's just that right now I feel such a big, sore emptiness that I don't even want to touch it. If I do, I might just give up. We need to keep going for each other."

Mary Ann curled even tighter into Olive's arms. Being huddled together felt better than any words Olive could say, and they watched silently as the men killed two of the cattle and butchered them, dividing up the pieces of meat into equal portions. They wrapped these into bundles to be carried with them—one parcel for each man. They roasted one large portion and made another batch of the burned bread.

The smell of roasting meat made the girls' stomachs growl, despite their fear.

It surprised Olive, as they ate, that no food had ever been quite so welcome as that piece of stringy beef and hard, ash-covered bread. She longed for sleep, but apparently the band of Indians planned to set out again without sleeping.

That day's journey became the hardest miles Olive ever covered. They set a punishing pace over rocky ground. Olive had become good at estimating miles covered. If they kept up the pace they would cover almost thirty-five miles in a day.

Before long, Mary Ann plopped down in the middle of the trail again, refusing to take another step. The man who'd been prodding her along stumbled right over the top of her. Furious, he began beating her again, but his blows didn't faze Mary Ann.

Olive thought she detected a grudging respect in the way he leaned down and hoisted her over his shoulder once again.

The Yavapai who'd been trailing Olive had her sit on a rock while he took dried grass and roughly wiped the blood off the soles of her feet. He stopped to remove some stickers and puncture vine thorns. Strangely, she'd never even felt them. He took some thick, hard leatherlike material and tied it onto the soles of her feet. It made the walking easier, though the flap-slap-flap of the makeshift sandal raised a lot more dust and she kept getting pebbles caught between the sole and her foot.

The men continued to watch the back trail, observing

much closer than Olive's fellow travelers had ever watched. It gave her a brief glimpse into the wariness and fear that marked these people. The threat of wagon after wagon of settlers must have weighed heavily on them.

At about noon, their path intersected with another band of about ten Indians—not Yavapai, maybe Apache. Olive noticed that while a group talked and gestured excitedly with the captors—mostly about her it seemed—two Indians came around behind. Olive saw one step out from the ravine. He leveled his bow straight at Olive and let an arrow fly. Mary Ann screamed, but Olive stood frozen. The arrow pierced her skirt and petticoat but did not injure her.

As the man reached for another arrow, several of Olive's captors jumped him and began clubbing him. Olive managed to figure out from gestures and Spanish words that the Indian had recently lost his brother to a white man and had vowed to kill the next settler to cross his path to avenge his brother.

The Yavapai fought the intruders and managed to send them running.

If anything, the pace quickened after that. They did not stop until about midnight, since the moon still shone bright and made night travel easy.

As Olive and Mary Ann lay down side by side, using their own blankets stolen from the Oatman wagon, sleep did not come right away. Looking up into the starry sky, Olive pointed out constellations to Mary Ann, reminding her of summer nights when they used to sleep outdoors in Illinois.

"See. There's the Old Dipper. Do you remember the time we were sleeping on the grass in the dooryard, and you jumped up to get the dipper out of the bucket to show Royce why it was called that?"

"I remember. Royce kept squinting his eyes trying to see which stars looked like a water dipper." Mary Ann was quiet for a long time. "Do you think that Royce is now seeing the stars close up?"

"I don't know. He'd sure enjoy exploring if he could." Olive wished she understood heaven and kept trying to remember what she'd learned.

• • •

The journey ended on the fourth day after traveling a distance Olive gauged to be about a hundred miles. As the group drew near to an Indian village, dogs came out to greet them, barking and yipping in frenzied excitement. Next came excited children and curious women.

At the sight of women, Olive felt relieved. Perhaps they'd find friends of sorts among their captors. One woman came very close, and Olive smiled at her. The woman seemed stunned. She pulled back and without warning spat in Olive's face. Another reached down and scooped up a handful of sand and threw it at Mary Ann.

So much for a friendly welcome.

8

The Ransom Price

The captors set Olive and Mary Ann atop a pile of brush and bark. Olive's mangled feet kept slipping, but she eventually managed to find a solid perch. Mary Ann clung to her sister's waist. Would they be burned at the stake, like Joan of Arc? None of this made any sense.

Confusion seemed to reign among their captors as well. To the chorus of barking dogs and screaming, chanting Indians, musical instruments were added. Some pounded on stones with clubs or blew animal horns; others pulled a small string—like a fiddle bow—across a piece of warped bark. The noise was deafening but rhythmic.

A line of dancers began to circle the pile. Some were naked. Embarrassed, Olive averted her eyes from them. Others wore blankets. Most of the women wore skirts made of bark and tied round the waist with natural twine.

The circle began to move at a dizzying pace. The dance itself seemed angry and violent. While circling, the dancers chanted a singsong cry. One by one, when they reached a spot in front of the girls that had been cleared of all grass, the dancer bent himself to the ground, yelling and gesturing wildly, slapping the ground and leaping into the air. Each one performed the same movement in turn. There was something wild and powerful about it. For Olive, fascination overcame fear.

Over the course of the captive journey, Olive had expected death many times. She surprised herself by finding that once you got used to the possibility, a sort of numbness took over. Each new challenge struck fear at first, but then, when she and Mary Ann settled into the situation, they found a way to make do. Perhaps she was learning to live moment by moment.

For this moment, however, she found herself curious about her new hosts. Looking around the camp, she saw what she took to be a temporary village—a collection of wigwams with smoke trailing out of each one. Some had a stack of root baskets outside; others had frames with skins stretched on them, drying in the sun. The ground outside the structures was packed hard and shiny. *Maybe these aren't so temporary. Can people really live with so little?*

The dance continued. When the dancers eventually lost interest and the festivities wound down, the girls were pushed off the pile. Apparently, they planned no burning. Instead a Yavapai woman managed to explain with a mixture of

Spanish, English, and gestures they were now slaves—*onatas.*

"Oh dear, does that mean they'll never let us go?" Mary Ann asked later, when they were alone.

"It does mean we are property," Olive answered. "Perhaps they will trade us for a ransom."

"Remember when we played Indians with Royce and his friends?"

"Yes. And you hated being held captive." Olive smiled to remember the way her little sister had screamed.

"You came and took my place because we had no ransom."

"I remember."

"Do you think someone may come and take our places?"

"Who, Mary Ann?" Olive often wondered if anyone searched for them. She remembered the night that Lorenzo promised that if any Oatmans were ever taken captive, he'd not rest until he rescued them. How she missed her big brother. "Anyone coming after us would carry along a ransom to trade for us, or else, if the army came, they might take us by force."

"When we played the game, why didn't you just come in and take me, like the army?"

"I didn't want to ruin Royce's game—I only wanted to get you free, so I played by the rules." Olive paused. "I got the idea of substituting myself for you from the Bible."

"They had Indians in the Bible?"

"No, silly. The idea of substitution came from Christ's dying. Remember?" When Olive saw the blank look on Mary

Ann's face, she continued. "When God put man into the world, everything was perfect."

"I know that part. Adam and Eve sinned and everything changed."

"That's right. Because of sin man had to die—we were all doomed. That's why Jesus came into the world. God's own Son became a man and substituted Himself. He died in our place. So we could live."

"I remember now. Ma used to say He paid the ransom-price for us."

Mary Ann must have continued thinking about this, because later, when they were gathering mesquite for the fire, she said, "Remember Beauty and the beast?"

"I hardly think you'd let me forget," Olive said, pulling playfully on one of Mary Ann's braids.

"Beauty ransomed her father with her own life, didn't she?"

"Hmmm, she sure did," Olive said. "You do know, little sister, that *Beauty and the Beast* is a fairy tale, right?"

"Of course." Mary Ann made a face at Olive. "I'm not a baby. It's just that it is like the story of Jesus in some ways."

Olive smiled at Mary Ann. Sometimes she was surprised by her little sister's understanding. "Remember that time when Ma read 'Beauty' to us?" Those days seemed like a different lifetime. "She said that folktales were ancient made-up stories to help people understand the true story of God. Ma believed that many myths and folktales grew out of the truth, but when people told them over and over the stories changed."

Olive looked over at the men sitting by the brush pile. "Do you think that the stories told by the Indians around the fire still have parts of God's story in them as well?"

"You mean even when the people don't know God anymore, their old stories may remember parts of Him?" Mary Ann tilted her head as she considered this.

"I don't know for sure, but maybe." Olive wished she could find some proof that God still dwelled in the Indian village.

As the months wore on, Olive and Mary Ann came to understand what slavery meant. The girls still followed their mother's lifelong practice of gathering together for prayer each morning before starting work. They worked from the time the sun rose until it set at night. Much of the time they dug with sharpened stones in the ground for roots—a staple of the tribe's diet—or collected any elderberries still hidden in the trees. The women treated them with scorn. The children sometimes came up and pinched them or slapped them for no reason. It didn't make sense until Olive realized that the Indian women and girls were treated the same way.

Near starvation was an everyday part of village life, but it was worse for women and girls since the meat was mostly reserved for the warriors. The very best ever offered to women was watery soup made from the cast-off parts of meat. During their time with this outcast group of Yavapai, Olive saw many girls who looked permanently stunted by starvation. Others died.

Olive and Mary Ann ached with hunger most of the time.

Spring turned to summer and still they grubbed for food. Many of the people ate insects and lizards, but Olive and Mary Ann were still not fast enough to catch these. They wondered if they'd be able to swallow them if they ever managed to catch them.

Olive often wondered why no one tilled the soil to raise food. After she learned the language she tried to ask, but her questions did not make sense to her captors. Food, they told her, came from hunting and gathering. Sometimes there was plenty and sometimes none.

Near the end of the summer, visitors came into the camp. Olive learned they were Mohaves who had come to trade. She became as excited as the Yavapai when she saw that they brought fresh vegetables to trade. How she hoped she could manage to finagle at least a few bites of these for Mary Ann.

Her sister had grown even thinner over the spring and summer. The frailty and the cough that had begun on the Gila Trail had only worsened since coming to live with the Yavapai.

When the girls met each day to pray, Olive tried not to worry Mary Ann by praying too long over her health, but in her heart Olive prayed about it all the time. The prayer they prayed over and over was always a version of this: "Heavenly Father, don't leave us. Somehow let someone know that we live. Please send someone to ransom us or to rescue us. Save us, Lord."

Olive would continue praying silently long after they started digging roots: *Save us before Mary Ann dies. Please, Father. Strengthen her. Let her know just one touch of kindness once again. Don't forget us, Lord. Where are You, oh God?*

After the girls learned the language and began to speak with their captives, they learned more about them. The Indians were still angry and distrustful of the settlers—or *Americanos,* the name given by the Mexicans—but the longer Olive and Mary Ann lived among them, the less the Indians treated the girls like slaves. They merged into the group—treated much the same as the other girls and women.

Olive knew that girls would get no vegetables—these would be saved for warriors. Lately, however, several men from the group who had taken them captive had begun to slip bits of food to Mary Ann, who had grown so thin. Olive even overheard one man saying that he'd take Mary Ann back to the *Americanos* if he hadn't killed her family. He seemed to understand that because of the massacre they were outlaws. It ended up that the girls were hiding with the Indians as much as they were captives of the Indians.

Soon after the visit of the Mohaves, Olive began hearing bits of conversation that led her to believe that she and Mary Ann might be sold to the Mohaves, but nothing came of it. Summer moved into fall. Game became more plentiful, and everyone ate better for a time. Olive and Mary Ann gathered basket after basket of berries and even found some wild grapes.

Eventually, Olive stopped hoping that someone would rescue them, and they even grew tired of plotting to escape. Perhaps Dr. Lecount never made it to the fort. Perhaps no one realized there were two girls unaccounted for. Perhaps no one cared or everyone figured them dead. Olive often thought about Ma's words—that God walked alongside them on this journey. She wasn't as sure anymore—why hadn't He heard their prayers for rescue?

Winter passed and just as the trees began to leaf out, word passed through the Yavapai that the Mohaves were coming to trade for the captives.

When the small band of Mohaves crossed the rise, Olive could see five men and one young woman. Walking through the camp and listening to the talk around her, Olive found out that the Mohaves and Yavapai had agreed to the trade on the last visit, and the Mohaves had taken the terms back to their chief, Aespaniola. The chief sent his daughter, Topeka, to either approve or cancel the agreement that had been made.

As they came closer, Olive could see that Topeka could not have been much older than Lucy; she was probably seventeen or eighteen years old. Topeka's shiny black hair hung in a smooth sheet down her back. Olive's hand automatically moved to her own matted braids. Since coming into the Yavapai village, she hadn't worried about grooming. Hair washing was a rarity. Olive always carefully checked their blankets to make sure they didn't catch lice, but, other than that, she was too busy working to worry about hair.

Topeka's face was beautiful—perfect, except for a strange tattoo running down her chin. And she had the same kind of lines on her upper arms. Olive couldn't help staring. What was that? Her skirt consisted of reeds woven into a braided waistband. It moved and rustled as she walked and seemed more graceful than the bark skirts of the Yavapai.

That evening, Olive and Mary Ann were summoned to appear before a gathering of the Yavapai men and the visitors. The men solemnly warned the girls to show respect since it was the chief's own daughter who traveled hundreds of miles to buy them—as if Olive didn't already know all of this.

Olive watched Topeka as she talked to the men. She spoke sparingly, but Olive was impressed with the woman's manner. It was soft and respectful, but her words were firm. Olive kept watching Topeka's face. Something in her eyes suddenly caused hope to rise in Olive's chest.

Despite Topeka's calm manner, the camp was in an uproar. Olive hadn't thought it would matter whether they stayed with the Yavapai or not. The men who killed her family, however, felt differently. Their arguments grew loud and heated. Some wanted to trade the captives, but those who captured them took great pride in owning these *Americano* slaves and wanted them to remain. All night long, the girls listened to arguing—sometimes in Spanish, other times in Yuman—as the Yavapai fought about whether or not to sell their slaves. The men who had killed the family and captured the girls argued the longest, but in the end they lost.

Shortly after the girls had been dismissed, Olive heard that Topeka approved the trade on behalf of her father.

● ● ●

"Olive?"

Olive had been sitting near the bark pile where they'd been taken when they first came into camp almost a year ago. "I'm here, Mary Ann."

"Ah-hotch-o-cama says that Topeka came to pay a ransom for us. Is that true?"

"I think so," Olive said. "Nobody bothered to tell us, but I've been listening."

"Oh dear, it's funny to see a girl in charge, isn't it?"

"Yes. For Indians, it is very unusual." Come to think of it, Topeka, for all her respectful ways, seemed very powerful—young and pretty, but very powerful.

"She's not paying the ransom with her own life is she?"

"No. She brought a ransom with her. Do you want to know what we are worth?" Olive smiled.

"Tell me."

"Two horses, a basket of vegetables, a few pounds of beads, and three blankets."

Mary Ann whistled to indicate that she was impressed.

Olive hadn't heard that whistle of appreciation since Illinois days. It made her smile again. "I'll admit, little sister, there was a time or two I would have traded you for half those vegetables and just one warm blanket!"

Mary Ann laughed and whacked Olive on the arm.

9

Ki-e-chook—
The Ransom's Mark

With almost no farewell, the girls took their leave. Olive looked back. The women sat near the bark pile as always, heads down—working . . . always working. The men stood at the far end of the village with their backs to the departing slaves. Only the little children stood at the edge of the circle and watched Olive and Mary Ann leave. The dogs followed.

The Yavapai killed her family and yet, Olive and Mary Ann had lived among and come to know them. Her feelings confused her. The Yavapai village along Date Creek had been their home for nearly a year. They had longed to escape, and now, here they were, leaving. Was the ache in Olive's chest caused by the prospect of traveling even farther away from civilization? Or was it something else too confusing to understand?

Topeka warned them that the journey to the Mohave village was a long one—several hundred miles. The Mohave traveled even faster than the Yavapai had when they journeyed into captivity a year ago. By the middle of the first day on the trail Mary Ann gave up. She sat in the middle of the trail, laboring to catch her breath. Her skin had paled. It felt clammy when Olive put her hand to Mary Ann's cheek.

"What is wrong, little sister?" Topeka halted everyone. She squatted down near Mary Ann.

Olive answered for Mary Ann. "My sister started coughing on the Gila Trail, even before we were captured. It was during your windbreak moon. Now another windbreak moon—another year—has passed, and she's grown even weaker from hunger and from the cough."

Topeka didn't comment, but she took soft skins and wrapped the girls' already-bruised feet.

"Is that better?" she asked.

"Thank you," Olive said.

Topeka turned to the men who accompanied her. "We shall travel as the desert terrapin instead of the eagle. You must take turns helping the little one."

The men grumbled at the slower pace, but Olive could see that they dared not argue with Topeka. It made Olive look hard at Topeka. After having lived with the Yavapai for a year, she'd never seen a woman treated with respect. She'd observed that Yavapai dogs were treated far better than the women and girls.

At night Topeka took out blankets and arranged a bed for all three of them together. Once, during the night, Olive had turned over expecting to find Lucy curled up with her and Mary Ann. Instead, she opened her eyes to find this stranger with markings on her chin and ropes of black hair spread across the blanket.

As they walked through the barren Mohave Desert, Topeka became much less like a stranger. Her kindness touched a forgotten place in Olive's heart.

"Why did you buy us?" Olive asked one morning. They had become comfortable conversing in Yuman, and Topeka was already teaching them her language.

"What do you think?" Topeka had a habit of asking a question instead of giving an answer. Olive thought it might have been because Topeka liked listening more than talking.

"Is it because you needed more slaves?"

"No. We have enough people in our tribe to do the work of planting and hunting."

"Is it because . . ." Olive didn't know how to say 'pride' in either tongue. "Is it because having slaves adds to your stature?" Perhaps that was close enough.

Topeka laughed. "No."

They continued walking. This was how conversations went with Topeka—few words and long pauses. Olive watched Mary Ann riding on the back of one of the men. At home they would have called it piggyback, but Mary Ann was obviously exhausted, maybe sleeping, and sort of hung down limply.

"I heard of the massacre shortly after it happened," Topeka said. "TokwaOa came to us to say that the Yavapai had captured a white girl named Aluitman."

"Aluitman?" Olive wondered if another family had been murdered and another girl taken.

"Listen to the way I say your name—Ah-lee Oot-man."

"Oh. Aluitman was me." So someone did know she lived. "What about Mary Ann?"

"We did not know about Mary Ann until our people went to Date Creek."

"When you went to trade?"

"Yes. Though we used trade as the reason to see about this Aluitman." Topeka walked silently for a while. A piece of her hair whipped against Olive as the winds shifted, swirling dust around the trail. "My father and my mother are good and wise. That is why my father is chief."

Olive kept walking. She knew if she interrupted with questions, the conversation might end.

"My father asked me if I had heard about this Aluitman. I told him I had. He never said any more."

Mary Ann stirred, wanting to stretch, and the man who carried her let her slide down to the ground. She dropped back and walked alongside Olive and Topeka. Olive could see Topeka's worried glance, but they both silently agreed to let Mary Ann walk a short distance.

"I could not get the idea of Aluitman out of my mind," Topeka continued. "Sometimes as I slept, I even dreamed about her—worried about her. I finally went to my father and asked if I could go to the Yavapai and see for myself."

"You did?" Olive felt a strange stirring at this conversation. For some reason she felt like crying.

"My father never asked me why I wanted to go. He decided to send warriors first. They could bring food for trade and go into their village to see if the stories were true and if the Yavapai would consider trading for Aluitman if she were there. During the time they were gone, I still dreamed of you."

Olive squeezed her eyes shut. Could this have been the answer to her prayers when she asked God to send someone to ransom them? Shivers ran along her shoulders. It was almost funny. When Olive had prayed, she pictured God mobilizing the army at Fort Yuma to make a daring rescue. Instead, God spoke quietly to a Mohave chief and his daughter.

"When the warriors returned, they told us about two white girls. They also told us that the Yavapai agreed to trade if we could meet their ransom price."

Topeka looked over as a snake slithered off a warm rock.

"My father agreed, but he wanted me to go along to make certain that no last minute tricks were played. It was too late in the year to travel by the time all was settled. The snows would have blanketed the mountains before our return. I had to wait until spring."

"So that's why so much arguing took place when you came with the men."

"Yes. We worried that they might agree to accept the

ransom price and then ambush our warriors and recapture you on the trail. With the chief's daughter along, they wouldn't risk offending my father."

Olive turned and looked at the back trail.

Topeka laughed. "We are safe, little sister. We have our own warriors trailing us."

"But you still risked your life to save us?" Olive could barely get her thinking around this idea. ". . . *and* you paid the ransom for us?"

"Actually my father paid the ransom price."

Mary Ann had been silent up to that point. "Oh dear, Olive," she said, poking Olive in the arm. "It's what we prayed!"

"Prayed?" Topeka asked. "You mean you asked our Great Spirit—the god who made all things?"

"I think so," Mary Ann said, not quite sure of herself. "Did that god send his son to pay the ransom price for you?"

"No. I do not think so," Topeka said. She sounded as puzzled as Mary Ann. "You need to tell me more about this God of yours who sacrificed His Son."

As they walked, Mary Ann told Topeka about God. Topeka listened.

Before long Mary Ann began falling behind, and Topeka called a halt in order to eat and rest. The warriors seemed impatient, but they did as Topeka directed. As they went off to find wood for a fire, Olive dug for roots to add to the *pinole* Topeka's men carried.

Topeka took the *pinole*—flour made of ground corn and

mesquite beans—and made small cakes to cook on a hot stone in the fire. With the mush made from the roots Olive gathered, they ate a satisfying meal.

The journey continued trouble free. The travel was difficult and even though Topeka had slowed the pace, they still covered more than twenty miles a day. On the eleventh day, late in the afternoon, they climbed one last steep hill. Mary Ann had to be coaxed and carried much of the way, but at the top, she stopped suddenly.

"Oh dear, Olive, look!" She pointed down into a valley carpeted in a rich green and rimmed by craggy peaks all around. The lower foothills were also covered in grass and wildflowers. "This is the place I want to live."

"What a beautiful valley, Topeka." Olive could see that the valley stretched for some twenty miles or so. To the right she saw low huts tucked in a nook in the hills near the banks of the Colorado River that ran through the valley.

"This is our home," Topeka said softly.

• • •

Coming into the village, the band of travelers was met by a running, laughing, dusty group of children. Songs, laughter, and clapping met them at every home. Topeka and the girls headed for the chief's home on the rise just overlooking the river by a grove of cottonwood trees. The house was set in an enclosure made of large peeled poles nearly twenty feet high. An opening in this enclosure formed the doorway and led to an inner grassy yard and a smaller, shorter enclosure with a reed-matted, mud-plastered roof.

How different this is from the Yavapai village, thought Olive. The biggest difference came in meeting Topeka's family. After her father quietly met Olive and Mary Ann, he turned to Topeka and hugged her, clearly excited to see her. Her mother couldn't stop asking questions, hugging and smiling. They loved Topeka.

The responsibility that seemed to ride heavily on the girl fell away. She laughed and danced around the inside yard, glad to be home. Inside she took a crusty cake of bread resting in the coals and broke it in three parts, giving Olive the largest. Nothing ever tasted as good. The girls ate every crumb.

Olive and Mary Ann spent the next few months—or moons, as the Mohaves counted time—discovering things about their new home. Patches of winter wheat grew in the valley. Instead of only hunting and gathering, the Mohaves tilled the ground. That made Olive happy because she thought it surely must mean more food.

As planting time came, however, the girls expressed dismay to Topeka at how the planting was done.

"Back home, our farmers could have planted acres with the same effort your people plant one hillock with five stalks of corn." Watching them exasperated Olive.

"My people plant in the ways of our fathers," Topeka quietly explained. "They must wait for the overflow of the Colorado to deposit rich soil. Then they take the seed gathered from the year before and plant it according to the moon."

"But if you grew more, you could collect more seed and grow more the following year," Olive said.

"We only want to grow what the land can nurture. We only want to grow what we need to fill our hungry bellies."

It frustrated Olive. She and Mary Ann were always hungry, and this was the time of the spring harvest. Topeka's needs and her needs certainly differed.

It was at times like these that Olive longed for home. She knew that her old home and even her family no longer existed. But home was the place you felt comfortable—where the ways were known—the smells familiar, the seasons predictable. It was where you understood the people—not just their language, but what they meant and where they got their ideas. She and Mary Ann remained strangers in a foreign land.

It was not that the Mohaves did not make her feel welcome. In fact, when Aespaniola introduced them to the tribe he put one girl on either side of him, put his hands on their shoulders and said: "Let all the people help raise them. If they fall sick, tend them. Treat them well." And, for the most part, the Mohaves treated them like part of the tribe. At first some of the children tried to boss them around, but one look from Topeka changed the children's minds.

Being treated like one of the tribe meant work, however —hard work. Both Olive and Mary Ann went back to gathering berries and digging for roots. They had to range far, since the scanty supply of roots nearby was reserved for the old women.

One morning, as they took their baskets and prepared to gather berries, Topeka stopped them. "Come with me to our house."

"Now?" Olive was surprised. No one stayed at home during the day.

"Yes. The physician has come to apply the *ki-e-chook*."

"*Ki-e-chook?*"

"The markings we wear on our chins. It is time for you and Mary Ann to get the mark. When we ransomed you, you became ours," Topeka said.

"You mean this is the mark of a slave?"

"No. You see I wear one. Am I a slave? Because you are ours, you are bound to us. We must protect you. If another tribe finds you while you are out digging roots, they will not hurt you when you wear our mark of protection."

Olive didn't know what to say. She didn't want the tattoo. It meant she would forever be different from her people. She wanted to go home, but if she had the *ki-e-chook,* she would always be different. She could never live unnoticed with one foot in each world—she would be forever marked as a child of the Mohave.

She looked at Mary Ann, standing silently beside her. Her sister did not cry, but her chin quivered and she hung her head. "Will it hurt, Topeka?"

"Yes, but you are brave, little sister."

It did not hurt as much as Olive supposed. They laid her down and the skin on her face was pricked with a very sharp stick in geometric patterns. The dye, made from a stone that could be found in the shallow parts of the river, had already been prepared. The stone had been burned until it crumbled easily into a powder and mixed with the juice from a weed that grew near the river. The pulverized rock dye was pressed into the pricked pattern on the girls' chins.

The doctor then pricked a line onto their upper arms and pressed the dye into the design. Getting the *ki-e-chook* didn't hurt as much as Olive expected it would, but for the next five days, the pain was intense.

Over the next few weeks, Olive kept trying to catch a clear reflection in a still pool on the river. When she finally felt she knew how it looked, she vowed to look no more. The *ki-e-chook* forever changed her. And to think she had worried about Lucy and Susan staining their lips with berries.

10

———

Famine and Peace

Time passed and Olive marked the seasons along with the Mohave. The spring gave way to a hot, dry summer. Hunger marked every day. The rains never materialized that first spring, and Olive learned that it almost never rained in summer in the Mohave valley. Parts of the river bottom dried and developed deep fissures. By autumn they harvested what little crops survived. Olive and Mary Ann gathered mesquite beans and dug for roots—much the same as they had with the Yavapai.

Olive watched Mary Ann and worried. She'd become little more than skin and bones. Her cough worsened.

"We have to find more food for you, Mary Ann." Olive knew the impossibility of this. They ranged farther and farther in their search for food. The Mohaves shared their food equally—not like the Yavapai who fed warriors first.

"Everyone is hungry, not just me," Mary Ann said. "I see

little babies who cry all the time. Oh dear, it breaks my heart."

"I know, but you are all I have—I want you to get better." Olive couldn't imagine life without her sister. She kept Olive connected to the past. Sometimes they still talked in English together, but even that slowly slipped away. And Mary Ann still dreamed of escape or being ransomed back to the States. Without her, Olive knew she'd soon settle for the routine of desert life.

Topeka and her mother worried about Mary Ann as well. More than once, Olive saw Topeka's mother break a little piece off her own portion and secretly pass it to Mary Ann.

The one hope that sustained them was the promise of coming rains. When it rained, the Colorado would flood, the land would once again turn green, corn and grain could be planted, and wild crops gathered. How they longed for rain.

Olive took to watching Topeka's face. In the early weeks of the dry spell, Topeka still seemed serene, encouraging the others and planning for the rain. As weeks stretched into months, Olive watched worry settle onto Topeka's brow in furrows, much like drought cut into the landscape.

Work increased for everyone as they ranged farther and farther to find food. Grain played out completely. The Mohaves subsisted on a mush made from mesquite roots that had been pounded to a pulp and mixed with water to cook up into a gooey, stringy lump. The mush filled a person's empty belly and helped stave off the worst hunger pains, but it didn't seem to have much nutrition.

Because of the drought, the hunters could no longer find game. During autumn that year, the ducks and geese never even stopped to rest from their migration south. The earth had been picked clean, and the marshes had dried.

Once, while out digging for roots, Olive and Mary Ann came across a man leaning against a tree. His skin looked like pemmican. His eyes were sunken. They remembered him from when they first came—he had been a bold young warrior then.

Olive ran to fetch the physician. After he examined the man, the doctor said there was little he could do. It was not disease, just starvation. This man's family had needed the food, and he hadn't managed to save enough to feed himself.

As he lay dying, his family cried. Olive wondered if they cried tears of regret. After he quietly slipped into death, his body was placed atop a stack of dried brush and burned, according to Yavapai custom. Those burning funeral pyres became all too common in the days to come.

One old woman remembered a grove of *tenatas*—trees— which once sustained their people in a long ago drought. Too old to go herself, she gave directions to the younger ones. When Olive learned it was a journey of nearly sixty miles over a treacherous mountain route, she begged Topeka to let Mary Ann remain in the village. Topeka agreed and promised to care for her.

Olive set off with a group of women. A few warriors came along for protection but little else. Carrying food was strictly women's work. Olive packed her empty *chiechuck,* the container that, with God's help, would hold the *oth-to-toa* berries.

They walked far beyond their strength. Several women sat down as if to await death, but friends always urged them on. After three days the party finally came to the place described by the old woman. They found the *tenatas,* which were really bushes resembling mesquite but with a much broader leaf. Some of these bushes grew as high as thirty feet but the *tenatas* were old and the fruit sparse. Those few berries that withered on the branches did little more than nourish the gatherers.

The taste surprised Olive. Even shriveled, the taste of the *oth-to-toa* berry was pleasant. When smashed and mixed with water it reminded Olive of the juice of an orange. The thought of finding more of these berries and bringing them back to nourish Mary Ann gave Olive renewed energy.

Dear God, let me find some young bushes. Please. I just know these berries will refresh Mary Ann. Guide me.

Olive emptied the few remaining berries into another woman's *chiechuck* and set off with a small party from their temporary camp in search of more berries. After wandering for two days, covering what must have been another twenty miles, they came upon a valley filled with the bushes. Olive and the women gathered berries to fill every single container. Since there were still so many left, each person ate as much as they could hold—trying to store up their own reserves for the continuing famine.

No one expected the berries to be so hard to digest. Within hours many writhed in pain. Olive's stomach seemed to squeeze in on itself until she could barely take a breath without pain. Some vomited, and others kept running for the forest to get relief. Olive's stomach settled down after a while, and she rallied enough to be able to bring water to the ones who still suffered. Three Indians became so sick they died of stomach distress. Since the others could not carry the bodies home, they built a funeral pyre right there in the valley of the *oth-to-toa* berries and sadly burned the bodies.

Having observed so much death, Olive returned to the village, dreading what she would find. When she saw Mary Ann with Topeka she experienced a mixture of relief at seeing her sister alive and despair at seeing that she'd become even thinner and more gaunt.

The berries gave a welcome, if temporary, relief. Topeka hoarded them and eked them out little by little.

Hope was even harder to find than food. Topeka's mother continued to try to slip extra bits of food to the girls even though her family starved as well. One day Topeka came to find Olive pounding the scant bits of mesquite root against a flat rock with Mary Ann sitting nearby. No one expected Mary Ann to work any longer—her weakness became more apparent each day.

"Come, sisters. My mother wishes to speak to you." Topeka reached out her hands to help them up. "Just leave your work, Olive, you can come back to it." No matter how grim their situation, Topeka smiled.

They walked toward the chief's house. Olive remembered worrying about meeting a chief all those months back when she first came. She had learned that the Mohave chief was a man respected by his people for his wisdom and fairness. Olive and Mary Ann had come to respect him as well.

But they had come to love Topeka's mother. From the very first she accepted them and cared for them. In the early days, when Olive tended to draw comparisons between the ways of Mohave farmers and the ways of the Illinois farmers, some Mohaves took offense. Topeka's mother just listened and smiled.

Now she stood smiling again. "Aluitman, I have a gift for you. You must keep it secret and guard it well." The chief's wife still called her by the Indian contraction of her full name.

Olive didn't speak. She couldn't imagine what Topeka's mother could offer. Since the famine, the Mohaves had precious little and everything they did have—like blankets and *chiechucks*—they shared freely already.

"Come." Topeka and her mother led her to a plot of flood plain near the river that had been marked off with stones. It was about thirty feet square. "This is the field for Aluitman and Mary Ann. You may plant your crops like they do in Ill-a-noy." She held out a bark pouch.

Olive opened the pouch and found seed grain—corn, melon seed, and wheat. She cradled the pouch in both hands.

Carefully hoarded seed represented the only hope of food for the future. This gift was given out of great sacrifice. Topeka's mother must have understood that Olive and Mary Ann needed hope more than anything.

Olive couldn't help herself—tears ran down her face.

The Mohaves prized emotional restraint, but Topeka's mother seemed to understand that Olive's tears welled up from a deep sense of gratitude. "You plant the wheat now to harvest in spring," Topeka's mother said. "Then, when Colorado floods and brings rich new earth, you plant corn and melon."

"Hide the corn seed," warned Topeka. "With so many of our people starving, it could be made into a mush that would feed a family for three days."

• • •

Each day the sisters toiled on their own piece of ground. Olive dug a deep hole near a rock and hid the pouch containing her spring seed. They spent hours tending the plot and praying over every shoot. Recently Mary Ann had started singing again. Now Olive would work as Mary Ann's thin voice whispered long-remembered hymns. If only Mary Ann could grow stronger. Olive didn't know how they could get by until harvest came.

Once after singing, Mary Ann said, "Olive, I think I'm going to die soon." She paused and then shook her head. "No. I already know I'll die, but you'll live and get away."

"Don't talk like that, Mary Ann!" Her calm frightened Olive.

"Oh dear, don't be sad for me, Olive," she went on as if Olive had not spoken. "I've been a burden for you. I hate to leave you all alone, but God is with you." Mary Ann's voice became almost dreamy sounding. "Our heavenly Father will keep and comfort those who trust in Him."

Olive didn't know what to say. She wanted to reassure Mary Ann, but her sister's words came from somewhere deep. Olive did not refute them with empty words.

"I'm so glad we were taught to love and serve the Savior, aren't you, Olive?"

Olive wished that, like Mary Ann, her faith grew stronger with trouble. Instead, she wondered where to find God in all this suffering.

Mary Ann drifted off into sleep soon afterward. Olive wrapped her in blankets and sat beside her. She no longer coughed, but her breathing seemed so weak. Sometimes she woke briefly to sing a piece of an old hymn. Many Mohaves stopped by to see her. To them it must seem so strange, this slip of a girl sleeping and whispering songs.

Topeka's mother came to sit with them. Putting her hand on Mary Ann's face, the older woman broke into sobbing. Olive looked at her for a long moment and saw the love and sense of deep mourning.

"Olive," Mary Ann's voice woke Olive out of a restless sleep that night. "Sometimes I remember the story of Beauty.

I keep thinking I can almost see Ma and Pa in a mirror. If I just close my eyes, I feel as if I could be there."

"Oh, Mary Ann, that was just a story."

"I know," she said smiling. "But I'm not afraid to go. I'll be so much better off there."

"I know, little sister."

Soon afterward, Mary Ann fell asleep for the last time.

11

War and Plenty

O live," Topeka shook her gently. "You must wake up."
Olive pulled the blanket around her shoulders and
tried to ignore the voice.

"Mary Ann insisted that you not grieve. I heard her request
that of you many times. You must respect that last wish."

Olive turned toward Topeka. "I want to respect Mary
Ann's memory, but I do not want to live without her. My sister went to be with our family. I am left here alone." Olive
began to cry. The tears surprised her. They were the first shed
since her sister died.

"The warriors prepared her body for burning, Olive. Won't
you be part of the ceremony?"

A new wave of despair crashed over Olive. Her whole
family had perished in the desert, left to the wolves, and now
Mary Ann—the sister who'd become so precious to her in

these years of captivity—Mary Ann was to be burned in a pagan ceremony.

Olive stood up, dropped her blanket and ran to the river. As her feet slipped on the rounded stones at the water's edge, she caught herself and shouted to the sky. "How can You let this happen, God? Even when Ma and Pa died, I continued to believe Ma's words that You walked alongside us." She reached down to pick up a stone. "The whole time we've been here, we've clung to You . . . hung on for our very lives." Olive's voice wobbled. "Mary Ann barely had enough strength to breathe in and out, but she sang hymns to You. How could You let her die?" She hurled the stone into the stream. Because the river ran so low, she heard a loud *thunk* as the stone hit the muddy bottom. "And why do You make me live?"

She picked up another stone, a jagged one, and flung it into the water after the first one. She threw another, followed by another. She kept casting rocks and weeping until her strength gave out and she sank to the ground.

"Come, sister." Topeka lifted Olive to her feet.

Olive had no idea how long she'd sat by the water's edge. She felt strangely comforted by Topeka's gesture.

"My mother wishes to speak to you. She needs your help."

Olive struggled to her feet, brushed the dirt off and followed Topeka without speaking. They went into the chief's yard where Olive saw a bundle wrapped in a beautiful Indian blanket. She knew that the blanket contained her sister's body. The pain in her throat threatened to choke her.

"Aluitman, my little daughter, I need your help." Topeka's mother took both of Olive's hands in her own work-roughened hands.

"I will help, Mother. What do you need?" The word *mother* seemed to come naturally after hearing Topeka use it for so long. It somehow felt right. Topeka's mother would never be Ma, of course—there would only ever be one Ma.

"The chief decided that our Mary Ann should be buried in the way of your people, not in the way of our people."

Olive stood stunned.

"He gives two blankets in which to wrap little daughter, but you must show the warriors how to plant her into the ground. We do not understand these customs."

Olive fell to her knees and kissed those worn hands. She could not put her feelings into words. *Is this You, Lord?*

A sad party carried that blanket-shrouded body out to the garden plot that Olive had so carefully tended that autumn and over which Mary Ann had so earnestly prayed. The warriors dug a grave about five feet deep and gently lowered the frail remains into the cavity, covering it with fine sand. It was the first and only grave in that entire valley.

Olive walked back to the chief's house beside her friend. Her grief was so deep; she still could not find words to speak to Topeka. Speaking seemed unnecessary; besides, she couldn't shake the feeling that the Lord walked unseen beside them. Even after she had screamed her frustration by the river's edge, Olive somehow sensed that the Lord had not left her.

As she walked along, she even looked at the sand once to see if there was a third set of footprints. *Forgive me, Lord, for doubting Your presence. I still don't know why You would allow such suffering, but when the chief offered a Christian burial for Mary Ann—a thing for which I never thought to ask—I saw that it was Your work. The chief's kindness broke my heart. Help it break my anger as well.* Olive continued to walk and think. *Despite what Ma said, God, I've felt so alone during most of this journey. My faith has been shaken. I need to understand.*

Hmm. She thought about that. If she really had faith, would she need to understand? How does one reclaim the blazing fire of faith when it's dwindled to nothing more than a wobbly wisp of a candle flicker?

Just ask.

That word intruded right into the middle of Olive's thoughts. Ask? She remembered Ma saying that faith was a gift—not something a person could ever attain. That made sense. At least she thought it did.

OK, I'm asking then, Heavenly Father. I may never understand why all this evil happened, but I'm all alone now and I don't want to live if I can't trust You. Trust is so difficult. I can't understand why You didn't save Mary Ann and me. We prayed so hard to be ransomed and rescued. Now Mary Ann is dead and I remain a captive. Olive's thoughts went in circles. One minute she reached out to God in faith and then the next minute asked, *Where are You?*

Olive saw that they drew near to Topeka's home. *Forgive*

me again, Lord. You tell me to ask for faith, and all I can do is cry out, "Why?" She took a deep breath and let it out slowly. *Please give me the gift of faith. I want to believe again.*

Topeka led Olive into the house and helped her lie down on blankets. As she closed her eyes she thought to herself, *I've obeyed that voice and asked. Now I need to figure out how to listen for an answer.*

• • •

Olive woke to a grinding sound.

Topeka's mother sat crouched by Olive, holding a grinding bowl and a wooden spoon filled with more than a handful of corn mush. "Eat this, daughter, and live. We have enough for you to eat for three days."

Olive sat up and ate her first nutritious meal in weeks. She'd grown too weak to even wonder where the corn for this mush had been found. By the second day, she began to revive enough to see that no one else had food—only her. Topeka's mother had ground this food for Olive and fed her, spoonful by spoonful, while the older woman continued to starve.

On the third day, Topeka came to bring the mush to Olive.

"No, Topeka. It's not right that I have a belly full when you and your mother starve."

"My mother wishes you to have this." Topeka pressed her lips together in that way that meant she would hear no more arguments.

"But why?"

"She longs for you to live, even if it costs her own life."

"Her own life?" Was Chief Aespaniola's family that close to death and Olive had missed the signs?

"Forgive me. I should have held my tongue, sister."

Suddenly Olive understood where Topeka's mother got the corn. The corn mush was made from the stash of seeds Topeka's mother had saved to plant in the spring. It represented the only flicker of hope for their entire family. Olive began to weep.

"Please, Olive, do not cry. My mother would not wish her gift to wound you."

Olive swallowed her tears. She took the bowl and ate—slowly and reverently. Through this sacrificial gift, Olive would live. She must find some way to honor Topeka's mother by her life.

• • •

That winter, the rains finally came and, in the spring, the banks of the Colorado River once again overflowed, depositing rich silt on the land. Wild game and fowl came back to the valley in time to stave off any more deaths from starvation.

With plenty of food and more crops in the ground, Olive looked for a sense of peace to settle on the Mohave valley. She was wrong. Part of the reason that peace had reigned the whole time she lived with the Mohaves was because finding food took up all their energy.

Topeka once told Olive that the Mohaves had fought the

Cocopas—a large tribe 700 miles away—for generations. The Mohaves believed they were destined to eventually conquer the Cocopas and had fought them many times—always winning.

When the first words of war crept into village talk, Olive became frightened.

"Topeka," she said while helping her friend hoe corn, "will they fight here in the village?"

"No. The warriors plan to leave on a raid tomorrow. They will go all the way to the Cocopa village."

"Then we are safe." Olive felt relieved.

Topeka did not answer, and Olive realized she might have seemed heartless. "I know our warriors are at risk, and we will worry. I just meant that immediate danger would not touch us here in the village."

Topeka's continued silence frightened Olive. "What, Topeka? Tell me."

"The thing I worry about may never come to pass."

"Tell me!" Olive's voice held a touch of hysteria.

"We have an ancient tradition that requires us to sacrifice a slave for every warrior killed in war. You must not worry, however, for our warriors are always successful."

"Sacrifice a slave? You mean kill someone?"

"Yes." Topeka stayed silent for a time. "The reason I tell you this is that some of our warriors argue with my father, insisting that you are a slave. Until all our warriors are back safe, you must stay by my side."

Olive began to shake.

"I did not tell you this, sister, to alarm you. I only want you to be on your guard." Topeka put down her hoe and took Olive's hand and pulled her down to a rock where they could both sit. "Do you not believe your God can protect you?"

Olive looked deeply into Topeka's brown eyes. "Sometimes I've doubted His protection."

"When Mary Ann died, in your grief, you forgot much."

"Forgot much?"

"Yes. Do you not remember how your God spoke to me about ransoming you? During that time, I was consumed by the urgency to rescue you from the Yavapai."

"I had forgotten." Olive mulled Topeka's words. "Oh, not that I forgot the great risk you took to ransom me, but I forgot that you told us you believed it was God's nudging." *How could I forget this proof of God's protection?*

"When my father called us together to say that he wanted your sister to be buried according to the custom of the white men, I suspected a Great Spirit planted that idea. I saw how much it comforted you."

Olive felt shivers run across her shoulders. "And when your mother gave me her corn seed to save my life?"

Topeka nodded her head. "Even the discovery of the *oth-to-toa* berries—our people believed it to be a great miracle." Topeka took Olive's hands. "Remember. That is what we tell our people. Remember and tell the stories of great deeds. If you keep remembering the great deeds of your God, you will see His protection."

Olive had asked God for faith. Maybe this friend who didn't even know God had the answer. Instead of asking why bad things happened, Olive needed to remember the miracles. She needed to remember the times the Lord took care of her and the times He whispered to others to take care of her. When Topeka recounted God's faithfulness, Olive saw what Ma had said all along—God walked alongside. Olive felt sure He had wept with her at Mary Ann's grave. Maybe the Lord had even remembered His own sacrifice when He watched Topeka's mother grinding corn.

12

The Final Ransom

O live!" Topeka shook her awake. "They are back."

"The warriors?" Olive shook off the last fuzziness of sleep.

"Yes. They are all back and you are safe." Topeka's voice rang with happiness. "You are safe."

The warriors returned with much ceremony. They had won again, and this time they suffered no losses. Topeka looked at Olive and smiled. *Yes,* Olive thought, *I'm beginning to see God's protection.*

• • •

Thinking that perhaps life would finally settle down to a quiet routine, Olive harvested her garden and stored up food against the winter. As she gathered the seed for the next year's crop, Olive couldn't help but recall God's care for her over the last five years.

She touched the tattoo on her chin. How disfigured she had felt when they first applied it. Now it no longer bothered her. It had become the ransom's mark—the remembrance of the price that had been paid for her by the Mohaves and their promise of protection. As Olive began to understand what God had done, and, as her flame of faith rekindled, she also liked to think about her *ki-e-chook* as the remembrance of the ransom price that Christ had paid for her with His own life and His promise of protection.

"Olive." The tone of Topeka's voice shook Olive out of her reverie. "Come into the house quickly. Trouble."

"What kind of trouble?" Peace never seemed to last very long in the valley of the Mohaves.

"A Yuma has come with a letter from the fort. It is written in English." Topeka shook her head in concern. "It is about you."

"About me?" If whites had known she lived with the Indians, why had it taken five years for them to contact her?

Topeka looked at her closely. "Do you know a man with a name something like Low-renz?"

Olive felt shivers run across her shoulders. "My brother's name was Lorenzo." She could never forget the last time she saw him—that horrible night—as he squeezed his eyes shut. Lorenzo . . . the big brother who always took care of them . . . who boldly promised that if they were ever taken captive he'd never rest until he'd rescued them.

Topeka hadn't spoken.

"Topeka?" The blood began drumming in Olive's ears. "Why did you ask about Lorenzo?"

Topeka took Olive's hand. "My father tells me that the Yuma—his name is Francisco—says that your brother, Low-renz, did not die in the Yavapai attack . . . that he has looked for you for all these years."

Lorenzo alive? Could it be? Olive thought back to that attack and remembered him being clubbed and falling to the ground. *Could he be . . . ?*

Olive came into the house, and Chief Aespaniola held out a letter. "Can you read it, Aluitman?"

She took the letter and read it aloud:

> *Francisco, Yuma Indian, bearer of this, goes to the Mohave Nation to obtain a white woman there, named Olivia. It is desirable she should come to this post, or send her reasons why she does not wish to come.*
>
> > *Martin Burke*
> > *Lieut. Col., Commanding*
> > *Headquarters, Fort Yuma, California*
> > *27th January, 1856*

Question after question came to Olive's mind—*Why now, after all this time?* If she did leave, where would she go? Wasn't she now more Mohave than white?

Was Lorenzo alive?

Chief Aespaniola worried aloud. "The Yuma not come at urging of white chief, Colonel Burke. Our people know scout at Fort Yuma. He say Colonel only agree to send short letter. A man, carpenter, the one they call *Carpentero*. He believe Low-renz, and he get Francisco to come trade for you."

She did not want to talk about the Yuma man or the people at the fort. It was too much for Olive to consider. *Lorenzo alive?*

The debate began right away. Topeka and her mother did not want Olive to go. They worried that the letter was a trap of some kind. They wanted Olive to stay in the safety of the valley.

But many of the warriors feared keeping her in the Mohave valley now that the soldiers knew her location. They didn't relish the idea of fighting the soldiers from the fort. Other Mohaves, who had come to accept Olive as one of them, were once again reminded she was an outsider. Olive felt a new wave of hostility.

Oh, Father, let them make the right decision. Olive knew the decision was not hers to make. What was the right decision? She knew she loved Topeka like a sister. But what if Lorenzo was alive?

The debate lasted for weeks, but Chief Aespaniola finally agreed to let Olive go. "You have become daughter to me and sister to Topeka, but if your brother lives, you need go."

Olive didn't know how to respond. As the drama swirled around her, Olive continued to work her garden patch, getting it ready for spring planting. Work kept her from worrying. *Oh, Mary Ann,* she thought as she turned the dirt over, *How I wish you were here with me. How I'd love to hear you sing one more time.*

The day finally came to leave.

Saying farewell to the chief's family nearly made Olive decide to stay. But she longed to see if Lorenzo lived.

"You will always have Mohave in your heart, daughter." Topeka's mother folded one of her blankets for Olive to take with her.

● ● ●

At least she did not have to say goodbye to Topeka immediately.

"I will walk with you as you travel back to your people," Topeka said.

"Oh, Topeka, it's such a long journey . . ."

"I must." Topeka looked hard into Olive's face, as if to memorize her. "My father still worries about you."

"I'm strong now. I can make this journey."

"He worries that treachery may be involved and this Yuma wishes to take you as his slave. When I see that you are safe, I will leave."

Olive looked at Topeka, her lips pressed tightly together. Once again, God had showed Olive His love through her Mohave friend.

They walked long distances each day over rough terrain and dry desert. Olive missed Mary Ann on this journey, even though the pace would have been too difficult for her little sister. She remembered her sister's words of so long ago—"I will die, but you will return."

As they approached the fort, Olive became quieter and quieter.

"What troubles you, sister?" Topeka finally asked.

"I wonder, to what do I return?"

Francisco sent an Indian running back to the fort to alert the soldiers that they camped nearby and would arrive on the morrow. As the runner came back to the camp, he brought a bundle for Olive.

Olive untied the twine and unwrapped the brown paper. Out tumbled undergarments, a corset, hoops, and a dress for her to replace her bark skirt. Olive turned the soft fabrics over in her hands, shaking her head. "Oh, Topeka. I don't belong to the white man's world any longer."

"It will take time. Just like when you came to us. Remember when all you could talk about was Ill-a-noy?"

"Yes. But my *ki-e-chook* means I will never fully belong to the white man's world. I do not think I can rejoin the people of my birth."

"As my mother says, Olive, you will always have Mohave in your heart. You need to remember that you belong to neither the Mohaves nor the whites. You belong to your God. He is the one who sent me to ransom you. He is the one who kept your brother alive and touched the heart of my mother and father."

Topeka wiped Olive's tears off her chin, gently tracing the lines of her tattoo. "Every time you look into the glass and see the *ki-e-chook,* you must remember God's love for you. It is the mark of ransom—of greatest love."

Olive heard the truth of Topeka's words. As Olive reached into the pile to pull a shift over her head, Topeka spoke.

"I take leave now, sister of my heart. I will tend the burial place of our sister for as long as I live."

Olive embraced Topeka, hating to let go. "Tell Chief Aespaniola and your mother that I will never forget their love and kindness."

• • •

Olive fastened the ties of the corset with clumsy fingers as she watched the figure of Topeka become smaller and smaller as she walked away from Olive back toward the Mohave village.

From somewhere deep inside her, Olive remembered bits and pieces of that psalm she had memorized all those years ago in Illinois: *"The LORD is my rock, and my fortress, and my deliverer; my God, my strength, in whom I will trust. . . . The sorrows of death compassed me, and the floods of ungodly men made me afraid. . . . In my distress I called upon the LORD. . . . He delivered me from my strong enemy, and from them which hated me: for they were too strong for me. . . . He brought me forth also into a large place; he delivered me, because he delighted in me."*

Yes, He had delivered her. She turned toward the fort to see a figure far in the distance—Lorenzo. As she stepped back into the world of her people, Olive knew that God would continue to walk alongside her.

Epilogue

Perhaps no saga of the journey west is more memorable than the story of Olive Oatman. When pioneers left the States to travel overland by wagon train they expected hardship and sometimes tragedy. The Oatman family, however, encountered catastrophe at every turn of their journey.

Olive Oatman's story is considered an important captive narrative because she recounted her ordeal in great detail and came to understand and respect the Mohave captors who ransomed her from the Yavapai. In 1903, ethnographer A. L. Kroeber interviewed the Yuma, TokwaOa, who accompanied Olive Oatman to Fort Yuma. TokwaOa's account yields rich detail about Olive's life among the Mohaves.

In her memoir, Olive calls their attackers Apaches, but according to ethnologists, they were of the Yavapai tribe—and, more specifically, an outcast, renegade band of the Yavapai who spread terror over the southwest United States and Mexican Territories.

Lorenzo Oatman survived the attack, and the story of his journey back to the Pima Villages is an adventure in itself. Soon after reaching safety, he was able to go back to the site of the massacre with the Kellys and the Wilders to bury his family. During Olive's five years in captivity, Lorenzo worked tirelessly to find his sisters, with almost no help from the United States Army. The attack occurred in what is now Arizona, but, because at that time it was part of Mexico, the event occurred outside of United States jurisdiction.

After the joy of being reunited, Olive and Lorenzo stayed with the family of Susan Thompson in California for a short time. They eventually left to rejoin their extended family. Several newspapers immediately carried the Oatman story, and the public clamored for more. Little more than a year after Olive returned, a clergyman, R. B. Stratton, wrote and published *The Captivity of the Oatman Girls,* with the help of Olive and Lorenzo.

Although Olive remained shy about appearing in public because of her *ki-e-chook,* she became a much-requested speaker—making appearances from coast to coast, including one in the New York birthplace of her mother, where the original Sperry lilac grew. She eventually fell in love and married, retiring from public life. She and her husband, Major John Brant Fairchild, settled in Sherman, Texas, and were lifelong members of St. Stephens Episcopal Church.

A plaque in LaHarpe, Illinois, marks the Oatman Lilac Bush in the LaHarpe City Park, started from a slip cut off the bush in the Oatman yard in Whiteside County, Illinois.

Olive's own words give vibrant testimony of her faith. In *The Captivity of the Oatman Girls*, when speaking of her narrow escape from death because of the success of the Cocopa war, she says: "I buried my face in my hands and silently thanked God. I sought a place alone where I might give full vent to my feelings of thanksgiving to my Heavenly Father. I saw his goodness, in whose hands are the reins of the wildest battle storm, and thanked him that this expedition, so freighted with anxiety, had issued so mercifully to me."

Mary Ann's words to Olive, recorded by her sister, stand as her testimony: "I shall die soon. I already know it. I shall die, but you shall live and get away. You cannot grieve for me. . . . I don't like to leave you all alone, but God is with you, and our Heavenly Father will keep and comfort those who trust in him. I'm so glad we were taught to love and serve the Savior."

Glossary

Adobe. Sturdy walls made with clay and straw.

Camaraderie. A feeling of friendliness.

Catastrophe. A terrible event.

Corset. Stiff hourglass-shaped fabric with wire or bone sewn in that was worn by women to shape their torsos.

Dooryard. The part of the yard closest to the front door of a house.

Emigrants. Those who move to a new country.

Gigot sleeves. Long sleeves that were very full, puffed at the shoulders, and narrow at the wrist.

Graniteware. Speckled, enamel-coated metal cookware.

Hoop iron. Long strips of iron used in barrel making.

Hoops. Also called hoop skirts, they were big round pieces of wire stitched into a slip and worn under a dress to make a woman's skirt bell-shaped.

Lay-abed. One who lies in bed too long.

Linch pins. Metal rods that fit into the axle to keep the wheel in place.

Mary Stuart cap. Small heart-shaped hat.

Mercantile. General store for groceries and other supplies.

Pemmican. Dried seasoned beef and berries pounded together.

Pinafore. A type of apron worn over a younger girl's dress.

Ruff. A large, round collar of pleated muslin or linen.

Skeins. Wound yarn or thread.

Slops bucket. Used as a nighttime toilet.

Stones. Refers to what Brewster called his "seer stones," used by him for fortune-telling and decision making.

Tableau. A scene that has been painted or represented using actors and props.

Theology. The study of God.

Toilette. Bathing, dressing, and grooming.

Wanderlust. A desire to travel to new places.

Watered silk. Silk cloth with a wavy pattern.

Acknowledgments

It takes a team to create a book. Special thanks to my gifted editors, Michele Straubel and Cessandra Dillon, as well as my agent, Janet Kobobel Grant. And thanks to Barbara LeVan Fisher for the beautiful *Daughters of the Faith* cover art. I owe another debt of gratitude to my brother, James R. Smith, for his hours and hours of library research and Internet genealogical work on the Oatman family.

A classic work of literature, adapted for children and beautifully illustrated.

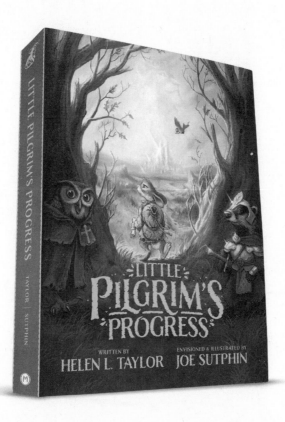

John Bunyan's *The Pilgrim's Progress*, adapted for children and beautifully illustrated. | *ISBN: 978-0-8024-2053-4*

Adventures, friendships, and faith-testers ... all under the watchful eye of a great big God.

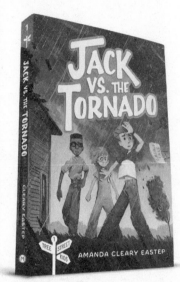

When Jack moves to the suburbs, can he get back to his farm? Or is God up to something else?

ISBN: 978-0-8024-2102-9

Can Jack and his friends protect his new puppy from Fang, a creature of the deep woods?

ISBN: 978-0-8024-2103-6

Daughters of the Faith Series

Ordinary Girls Who Lived Extraordinary Lives

Almost Home: A Story Based on the Life of the Mayflower's Young
MARY CHILTON | ISBN: 978-0-8024-3637-5

The Captive Princess: A Story Based on the Life of Young
POCAHONTAS | ISBN: 978-0-8024-7640-1

Courage to Run: A Story Based on the Life of Young
HARRIET TUBMAN | ISBN: 978-0-8024-4098-3

Freedom's Pen: A Story Based on the Life of the Young Freed Slave and Poet
PHILLIS WHEATLEY | ISBN: 978-0-8024-7639-5

The Hallelujah Lass: A Story Based on the Life of the Young Salvation Army Pioneer
ELIZA SHIRLEY | ISBN: 978-0-8024-4073-0

Little Mission on the Clearwater: A Story Based on the Life of Young
ELIZA SPALDING | ISBN: 978-0-8024-2494-5

Ransom's Mark: A Story Based on the Life of the Young Pioneer
OLIVE OATMAN | ISBN: 978-0-8024-3638-2

Shadow of His Hand: A Story Based on the Life of the Young Holocaust Survivor
ANITA DITTMAN | ISBN: 978-0-8024-4074-7

The Tinker's Daughter: A Story Based on the Life of Young
MARY BUNYAN | ISBN: 978-0-8024-4099-0

ooks for kids from  MOODY Publishers® | *Books Kids Love and Parents Trust*

Christian classics for kids from beloved author Patricia St. John

---

Rainbow Garden

A secluded garden in Wales becomes a surprise solace for Elaine, a little girl traveling far from her London home. | ISBN: 978-0-8024-6578-8

The Secret at Pheasant Cottage

Lucy has only known life with her grandparents at Pheasant Cottage. So what are her dim memories of something—*and someone*—else? | ISBN: 978-0-8024-6579-5

Star of Light

Hamid and his little blind sister attempt to escape their mountain village and the threat of losing each other in search of a new home. | ISBN: 978-0-8024-6577-1

The Tanglewoods' Secret

Ruth and her brother, Philip, find solace and adventure in the natural beauty and mystery of Tanglewoods. | ISBN: 978-0-8024-6576-4

Three Go Searching

When Waffi and David, a missionary doctor's son, find a sick servant girl and a mysterious boat, an exciting adventure begins. | ISBN: 978-0-8024-2505-8

Treasures of the Snow

After Annette gets Lucien into trouble at school, he decides to get back at her by threatening the most precious thing in the world to her: her little brother, Dani. But tragedy strikes first. | ISBN: 978-0-8024-6575-7

Where the River Begins

Ten-year-old Francis is taken in by a new family while his mother is terribly sick. There he discovers the source of both the nearby river and the Christian life. | ISBN: 978-0-8024-8124-5

ooks for kids from MOODY Publishers® | *Books Kids Love and Parents Trust*

Heroines Behind the Lines Series

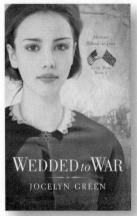

ISBN: 978-0-8024-0576-0

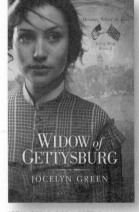

ISBN: 978-0-8024-0577-7

ISBN: 978-0-8024-0578-4

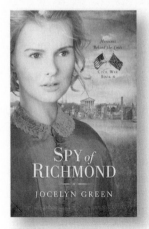

ISBN: 978-0-8024-0579-1

MOODY
Publishers

From the Word to Life